Blood Secrets
VIVI ANNA

WITHDRAWN

MILLS & BOON
Pure reading pleasure™

All the characters in this book have no existence outside the
imagination of the author, and have no relation whatsoever to anyone
bearing the same name or names. They are not even distantly inspired
by any individual known or unknown to the author, and all the
incidents are pure invention.

First published in Great Britain 2009
by Harlequin Mills & Boon Limited,
Eton House, 18-24 Paradise Road, Richmond, Surrey TW9 1SR

© Tawny Stokes 2007

ISBN: 978 0 263 87303 0

46-0609

Harlequin Mills & Boon policy is to use papers that are
natural, renewable and recyclable products and made from
wood grown in sustainable forests. The logging and
manufacturing processes conform to the legal environmental
regulations of the country of origin.

Printed and bound in Spain
by Litografia Rosés S.A., Barcelona

ABOUT THE AUTHOR

A vixen at heart, Vivi Anna likes to burn up the pages with her original, unique brand of fantasy fiction. Whether it's in the Amazon jungle, an apocalyptic future, or the otherworld city of Necropolis, Vivi always writes fast-paced action-adventure with strong independent women that can kick some butt, and dark delicious heroes to kill for.

Once shot at while repossessing a car, Vivi decided that maybe her life needed a change. The first time she picked up a pen and put words to paper, she knew she had found her heart's desire. Within two paragraphs, she realised she could write about getting into all sorts of trouble without suffering any of the consequences.

When Vivi isn't writing, you can find her causing a ruckus at downtown bistros, flea markets, or in her own backyard.

For all those amazing people who
continue to believe in me...

And for Shayla who constantly lights up my life.

Chapter 1

Where was all the blood?

That was the first thought that raced through Caine Valorian's mind as he entered room 210 of the Black Heart Hotel in downtown Necropolis.

The young woman on the bed had her throat slit from ear to ear. Besides the blood splatter on the graying wall behind the bed, there wasn't another drop on the green shag rug or the mustard-colored comforter. Not on first inspection anyway. Maybe with the ALS, alternate light source, he would find traces of it here and there. But for some reason that bored into his mind like a thumbtack, he doubted it.

Immediately, Caine could tell that this case was going to be different. After attending hundreds of cases over the past ten years, he knew when something was amiss, something odd and out of place. For a murder in the undead city of Necropolis, that was definitely saying something.

Popping a breath mint into his mouth, he approached the bed and nodded to Dr. Givon Silvanus, the medical examiner for the Otherworld Crime Unit, OCU, as he wrote notes in his logbook.

"Lividity is fixed, rigor in her jaw, neck and shoulders. I'd say she's been dead from six to eight hours," Givon stated in his matter-of-fact way without looking up from his notebook. "She's all yours."

Caine glanced back at his team, who were anxiously pacing behind him, waiting for the go-ahead to examine the body and collect the evidence. Jace Jericho had already taken multiple pictures of the hotel room from every angle, and now he was eager to inspect the body, as there were indications of possible bite marks, his specialty. Someone didn't live their entire life with lycanthropy and not know about the damage a set of teeth could do.

Lyra Magice had just finished inspecting the magical symbols etched on the door frame to the room. Her first inspection ascertained that there were no harmful magical blocks on the door to prevent them from entering, so the team had been allowed in. She also found bloodstains about knee-high on the doorframe and swabbed it for later analysis.

She was chomping at the bit to get to the body. They were told there were more symbols written in a red substance, most likely blood, on the young woman's chest. Having a full-blooded witch on staff had its advantages, especially in cases like these. Caine was eager to see what his youngest team member could do.

Having been together for the last six years, a brief nod from Caine was the only indication Jace and Lyra needed to move toward the body and begin their evidence collection.

"Lyra, make sure you look for trace evidence first before you inspect the symbols. I'd hate for us to miss something important."

She nodded and took out a magnifying glass from her stainless-steel crime collecting kit.

Before Caine could join them at the body, Captain Mahina Garner of the N.P.D., one of Necropolis's finest, strode into the room with the swagger of someone very comfortable in her five-foot-ten, 160-pound muscular frame, made even more powerful by her lycan shape-shifting abilities.

"The hotel attendant is an idiot," she remarked as she sidled up next to Caine. "He's a dumb blood-sucker that doesn't know the difference between his ass and a hole in the ground." She smiled at him then, straight white teeth gleaming. "No offense."

Caine smiled back, accustomed to Mahina's gruff manner and her prejudice against vampires. "No offense taken. I know my ass from a hole in the ground."

She laughed and patted him roughly on the back. "I know. That's why you're the only one of *them* that I like."

"Any witnesses?"

"Nope. No one heard anything. No one saw anything."

"Not surprising in this neighborhood. The Digs is not the most pleasant of places to be living and working."

She nodded. "True, but for once it would be nice to be able to start with something."

"Any ID on the body?"

"No." She opened her notebook. "The attendant phoned 911 after he realized he had no more rooms to rent for the hour, and noticed the do not disturb sign on 210. So he used his master key and opened the door to find, quote, 'the bitch lying on the bed dead,' unquote."

"Did he notice her when she went into the room?"

"No. He said he went on a blood break at around 10:00 p.m., and didn't notice the room's do not disturb till around 5:00 a.m., opened the door, saw the body and that is when he called 911." She closed the notebook. "So far his story checks out."

Caine glanced at his watch. It was 6:00 a.m. According to Givon's estimation, the girl had died around midnight. Therefore, if the girl and her assailant had come to the room during the time the clerk was on a break, they would have been busy for two hours before she died. What would you need two hours for? Sex? Likely, as the girl's shirt and bra were torn apart and her skirt was hiked up to her thighs. He didn't need to possess extreme sensory skills to smell the scent of sex as it still lingered over the bed.

Caine looked back at his crew working the scene. "What's the word, Lyra?"

"I pulled some burgundy fibers from her shirt, a tiny piece of what looks like copper wire and a black hair from under one of her nails."

"Good work. How about the markings?"

She glanced up from inspecting the woman's bare chest and the obscure symbols drawn there and met his gaze. Worry crossed her petite features. "Not sure yet, Chief. I don't recognize any of these symbols offhand. I'll need to get pictures and reference them to my textbooks." She held up a cotton swab, its tip tinged in pink indicating blood evidence. "It was definitely drawn in blood though. The vic's, I bet."

"Can you ascertain a magical signature from it?"

She scrunched up her face and cocked her head. "I'm trying but it's nothing I've seen before."

"Okay, just log it, and we'll search the signature log when we get back to the lab."

She nodded and went back to work on deciphering the symbols.

"I've got a set of bite marks on the neck," Jace said from his kneeling position beside the woman's head hanging over the edge of the bed.

"Are you sure?"

"Yup. The knife wound tries to mask it, but I can see a partial puncture into her carotid artery. There is no doubt that someone with fangs sucked on this girl's neck."

"Swab everything. Maybe we'll get lucky and find some DNA on that partial puncture. Hopefully our guy is a secretor."

"Aren't they all?" Mahina remarked.

Caine ignored her and continued to watch his team, observing them and the scene itself.

"At the lab, after we clean up the wound, we'll try and get a bite radius. Maybe we'll find a match in the computer log."

Jace swabbed the victim's neck, wound track and the blood spray on the wall. He glanced back at the body and ran a thick hand through his shaggy mop of dark-brown hair. "She was definitely bled out."

Caine took a step toward the bed and stared down at the rug. "But where's the blood?"

"Maybe the perp drank it all," he suggested.

Caine shook his head. "No. The average vampire can only consume a pint of blood without getting sick or passing out. If our guy drank more than that, there would be vomit everywhere or he'd still be on the floor in a druglike coma."

"Maybe he took it with him," Mahina suggested from the sidelines.

Nodding, Caine had thought of that. The blood had to have gone somewhere. "That's a lot of blood to carry out. He would've needed a couple of containers."

"He used something from the room?" Jace proposed, as he glanced around the scene.

Caine also looked around the room. There *was* something out of place. He had noticed it on his initial perusal of the scene. Out of place, or something missing.

He moved toward the little vinyl-covered table in the corner and its matching red vinyl chair. The table was suspiciously clean and devoid of any items that most used hotel rooms had. Ice buckets, used glasses, wrappers or other food items. He looked down at the ground beside the table. And what was in the room that a hotel guest would use to dispose of some of these items? The garbage can.

He rushed into the adjoining bathroom, which was more like a little closet with a toilet in it. No garbage bin there either.

"Garbage cans. They're missing," he announced as he came out of the washroom. "Someone check another room for the trash can."

"I have the master key." Mahina held up a key ring. "I'll go check."

Mahina came back into the room with a rectangular garbage pail under her arm.

Jace nodded then frowned. "How could one guy get two of those, full of blood, out of the room without anyone seeing him, and without him spilling it all over the place?"

"Maybe there were two of them," Caine suggested, his stomach twisting at the implications of what he just said. One rogue vampire killing people was bad enough, but two? It seemed unlikely as vampires preferred to roam alone rather than in groups. However, stranger things had happened.

It would be a huge issue in the community and could cause panic among the other races. Not counting the renewed panic in the human cities, if it leaked out that a vampire was on the loose killing people. The city was well guarded, behind the facade of a military base, but humans were a jumpy lot. It didn't take much for them to start a worldwide panic, especially when most of humanity had no idea that the undead city of Necropolis even existed.

"It looks like we have a problem," Mahina said.

"It's worse than that."

Everyone looked over at Lyra, who was still standing over the body, big brown eyes wide with wonder. She had a small clear vial in her hand. The liquid inside was blue, a bright sapphire-blue.

A color Caine recognized instantly as a huge warning and a problem he thought he'd never see in Necropolis. One he hoped he'd never see.

"The vic's human."

Chapter 2

"Nothing yet from DNA or trace," Jace commented the moment he stepped through the swinging metal door of the autopsy room, intense brown eyes smoldering above the blue paper face mask he wore.

Caine glanced up briefly as his second in command came swaggering up to stand next to him at the metal table. "You can take the mask off, Jace. She's dead."

"Yeah, but humans carry diseases. I don't want to catch anything."

Caine sighed and shook his head.

Jace rubbed his gloved hands together eagerly. "Are we ready, Sil?"

Givon stared at Jace, his steely gray eyes narrowing in question. "Eager are we, young man?"

"Hey, when do we *ever* get a chance to autopsy a human?"

Caine shook his head at his protégé's enthusiasm. "This is one time too many. When the human populace catches wind of this, there's going to be hell to pay. As if we don't have enough problems just trying to exist peacefully with each other. A confrontation is one problem we can't afford."

"I don't suppose we have an ID yet?" Jace asked.

"We don't have access to the human AFIS, so no, we don't have an ID yet."

Caine looked down at the young woman on the table. Even tinged gray, he could tell that she had been very pretty once. Well-groomed, fingernails and toes manicured, legs and pubic area freshly waxed. This girl was no criminal. She had been wearing designer clothing and expensive shoes when they found her. Likely, she was a girl from the right side of town, looking for a thrill, something shocking to stick it to her parents and show off to her equally well-bred friends.

She found it all right. The shock of a lifetime. Death by vampire.

"Was there evidence of rape?" Jace inquired.

"I did a kit and sent it into the lab." Givon's eyes narrowed. "She had sex, but there's no evidence that it was forced. No bruising or damage to her cervix." He picked up one of her dainty hands. "There was no evidence of skin under her nails, and no defensive wounds."

"So she willingly had sex with a vampire," Jace stated.

Givon shook his head. "Maybe not. I sent her blood to tox for drugs."

"Maybe she wanted to make a statement, piss off her parents. Who knows?" Caine offered. "We won't know anything until we can identify her and speak to her family and friends."

Jace snorted. "Oh, like the San Antonio Police Department will let that happen. We won't get within two miles of the city before human cops will be all over us."

Caine nodded, knowing Jace was right. The human populace on a whole wasn't aware of the existence of any Otherworld community, let alone a city built just for them fifty miles outside of San Antonio, Texas, behind the chain-link fence of a supposed military installation.

Fondly, Caine could still remember when heartthrob and two-time Oscar nominee Liam Wolf revealed on David Letterman that he was indeed his namesake—a wolf. In front of millions, Liam shifted into his animal form. Then he went on to explain about the pros and cons of lycanthropy. It wasn't long before it became cool to be a werewolf, and like magic, others stepped out of the shadows and declared that they too had the condition.

The government quickly contained the situation before anyone else could admit to being "different." News reports went out with scientific evidence of such a disorder, and cautioned people not to panic, as it was rare and not something from their nightmares and horror movies.

A few people with lycanthropy, especially one as

famous and glamorous as Liam, the world could handle. However, a hundred thousand with rare, strange and even dangerous gifts proved way too treacherous to let roam around the world unguarded and unchecked.

Under pressure from a certain powerful U.S. senator, who was rumored to be hiding a witch son, the idea to create an Otherworld city, aptly named Necropolis, was spawned. "For their safety," the city's supporters spouted. Although it was never determined which *they* was meant—the Otherworlders or the humans.

To this day, the city wasn't on any map. Only those with their eyes wide open knew of the city's existence. And that was very few people indeed.

"What else, Givon?"

"Her throat was cut with a serrated blade and her blood was siphoned with quarter-inch rubber tubing inserted into one of the bite holes."

"Sounds like our guy is knowledgeable in blood handling," Jace stated.

"All vampires know how to handle blood, Jace," Caine said. "If we didn't, we would die."

"Have you received a call from the baron yet?" Givon asked as he prepared to start the Y incision.

Caine patted his pants pocket to ensure that his dreaded cell phone was still there. He had it on vibrate, and so far nothing had hummed against his leg. "No."

"You will." Givon winced, as he cut into the young woman's chest just below her left clavicle.

He knew why Givon cringed. No one liked getting

calls from Baron Laal Bask. He was a young, wet-behind-the-ears vampire with delusions of grandeur who had been handpicked by the Mistress of the City, an overbearing, manipulative vampire a few hundred years older than Caine. Laal became her direct link to the crime unit and police force in Necropolis as a way to keep her thumb on the pulse of the city. A situation the baron continually pointed out every time he spoke with Caine, thinking that he had wanted the job for himself. The last person Caine had ever wanted to work directly for was Lady Ankara Jannali.

"Yes, well, eventually she will need to become involved. We'll definitely need a liaison between our community and the human one if we want to solve this case." Caine sighed, knowing somehow that he was going to carry the weight of this case around and deal with the consequences.

Three hours later, Caine sat in his small, cramped office and went over the evidence they had obtained so far. Haunting, melodious strains of a vampiric aria floated from the speakers of his office stereo. Sung by Nadja Devanshi, his preferred chanteuse, *The Crimson Moon* was his favorite opera. Everything seemed clearer when he listened to her poignant voice.

Right now, he had a need for some clarity.

Oddly enough, he hadn't received a call from the baron's office. Maybe the warnings he gave his people about keeping their mouths shut in the lab had worked this time around. Maybe this time, if he prepared himself quickly, he could be the one calling the baron with the bad news, instead of the other way around.

He flipped through his pages of notes and through the evidence log. The autopsy had gone as planned, with nothing showing abnormal. The COD on the girl was exsanguination. No surprise there. Her carotid artery had been punctured, her throat then slit and she bled out. They were still waiting for the results on her rape kit and toxicology. Caine suspected that they would find XYV, vampire sperm. Sex was very closely linked to bloodlust in the vampire community. For the most part, a vampire could control it. If a case of bloodlust came over a vampire, he or she could engage in sexual activity and the hunger would pass, replaced by rapturous sexual pleasure for both partners.

It had been over five years since they'd had a vampire slaying in Necropolis. And that case had been proven accidental. The perpetrator had been sentenced to three years in jail for the accidental killing of his witch lover.

Running a hand over his face, Caine wondered if they had a re-offender on their hands. He'd have to check his case journal, look it over and call Mahina to look up the vampire and question him to see where he'd been over the past twenty-four hours. Caine hoped not. During the case, Caine had ended up liking the quirky vampire. He'd really hate to have to put the guy back in jail.

Perhaps the offending vampire had acquired some

of his dead lover's spells. The markings on the door frame of the hotel room and on the victim were definitely magical. Lyra had gone through her texts she had packed into the small shelf in Caine's office, but couldn't find what she was looking for, so she asked to go home. She had archaic texts there in her extensive magical library. Some of her books, she claimed, were two thousand years old, and passed down to her from her grandmother. So far, Caine hadn't heard back from Lyra.

Unfortunately, they weren't able to get an accurate bite radius measurement. Therefore, they couldn't hit the OBRN, Otherworld Bite Radius Network, a database with all former vampire and lycanthropy bite offenders—a system Caine had developed himself. When a perpetrator was arrested, their fang circumference was measured and their tip-to-tip length recorded. Just like fingerprints, vampires and lycanthropes had individualized bite marks. If they could've matched that, they would've had a suspect. However, as it stood, the knife wound ruined any chance of an accurate measurement. *Maybe the perp's bite was on record and that's why he slit her throat?*

This case definitely had the makings of a disaster. For all the communities. What did a vampire, human and witch possibly have in common? What was this young girl doing in Necropolis with a vampire?

It was illegal for a human to be in the city. The city crossings, all four of them, were like border controls, and everyone coming or going had to produce

identification. But so far, there had been no record
of a young human girl crossing the borders. Caine
had them check every point of entry around the city.
And no one reported seeing or recording anyone
fitting the victim's description. So how did she get
into the city? Smuggled in? Most likely. But why?
For the sole purpose of killing her? If so, they had a
larger problem than just one murder.

The pager on his desk by the stacks of paper
suddenly buzzed. Caine picked it up and checked
the number. It was the lab. Hopefully, it would be
some good news. Maybe the lead they desperately
needed.

Caine stepped out of his office and strode down the
long, drab hallway to the lab. When he entered, Jace
was already there, sitting on one of the vacant chairs.

"What do you have?" Caine asked.

Gwen McKinley, the lab technician, raised her
plastic goggles and set them on top of her head. She
turned her intense blue eyes to Caine and frowned.
"I pulled two different strands of DNA from the kit
Givon sent me."

Jace nodded, excitedly. "So, there were two perps."

The report that had been sitting on the printer
suddenly lifted in the air and floated over to Caine.
He snatched it from the air. Gwen had strong tele-
kinetic power for a witch and often used it in the lab.
Sometimes it was like having two separate techs
doing the work.

Caine glanced over the report. XYV. Vampire
sperm present. No surprise.

He handed the reports back to Gwen. "Okay, so we have two suspects that the victim willingly had sex with."

"Well I wouldn't say that." Gwen handed him another report. "Tox came back. Vampatamine and heparin."

Caine glanced over the report. He shouldn't have been surprised. The drug vampatamine, or street name V, was an illegal substance produced from vampire saliva. It had the power to sedate and paralyze the user. A person wouldn't be able to move on V, but he or she would be completely aware of what was going on, or being done to them.

Heparin, on the other hand, did surprise him.

"They used the anticoagulant to make the blood flow faster," Jace suggested. "They wanted to be out of there quick as they could. Bleeding her out would've taken several hours if they hadn't, even with the rubber tubing."

"They wanted to keep the blood from clotting." Caine paced the lab, the sheet of paper rattling in his hand. "They needed the blood for later. How they got it is what we need to know. Who would have access to heparin?"

"Pharmacists, paramedics, anyone that works in a hospital," Gwen offered.

"That's a lot of people," Jace said. "Plus they could have stolen it."

Caine nodded. "Check to see if there have been any pharmaceutical break-ins or hospital thefts reported."

As Jace flipped open his phone to make the call,

Caine thought about the implications of the information they just received. A human in Necropolis.
Humans consorting with Otherworlders. The possibility of two vampires conspiring together to commit
murder was baffling. It would be a first, as vampires
were naturally solitary creatures. If that were the
case, and he prayed that it wasn't, how could they
solve this crime when there was no possible way that
Otherworlders and humans could work peacefully
together? There was too much fear there, too much
hatred. From both sides.

His cell phone took that moment to vibrate in his
pocket. He didn't need to be psychic to know that
Baron Laal Bask had beaten him to the punch again.

Caine flipped open the phone. "Valorian."

He listened for a moment, not getting a chance to
say anything. After a few minutes, he flipped his
phone closed and slid it back into his pocket. The
situation had just taken a turn from bad to disastrous.

"What's the word, Chief? Do you have to make
an appearance in the baron's office?" Jace asked,
with a chuckle. He wouldn't miss a chance to bug
Caine about his ongoing feud with the baron.

Caine turned toward his team and rubbed his eyes
with his fingers, a headache starting to brew. "Get
ready, my friends." He licked his lips and met their
gazes. "They're sending in a liaison on this case
tomorrow. A transfer from another lab."

Jace frowned. "But there isn't another lab in
Necropolis."

"No, but there is in San Antonio."

Jace jumped out of his chair. "We're getting a human in our lab?"

Caine just nodded. He was too disconcerted to voice an opinion, as of yet. The news was still trying to sink in. He had thought he was finished dealing with the human race. Had hoped.

"Why don't they just stick pins in our eyes? It would be easier to deal with." Jace paced in front of Caine, his shoulders hunched and his hands clenched angrily.

"I'm sure it won't be that bad, Jace," Gwen commented.

"Like hell it won't be." Jace turned and snarled at Gwen. "I pity the poor sap that walks into this lab. He has to have some big balls to think he can just stroll in here and be welcome. Because I don't play well with humans."

Caine eyed his team member. No, none of them played well with humans. They all had their sad, sordid histories before coming to Necropolis. A human had wronged every single one of them in some way. However, they needed help if they were going to solve this case and avoid persecution from the outside world. If this human had the resources to help them, he would take it, regardless of how he felt.

Chapter 3

Eve Grant walked down the drab hallway with her chin up. The soft clink of her high heels echoed off the graying walls. Tucking a stray blond hair behind her ear again, she tried not to stare at her two beefy lycan body-guards and the vampire baron walking ahead of her.

He glanced over his shoulder at her and smiled, his straight, white, elongated fangs flashing at her. She gave him a half smile. Why did she ever volunteer for this job? She was not strong enough for this. No research in the world could have possibly prepared her for what she was getting herself into. Why did she have to open her big fat mouth at the emergency lab meeting and say that working in the OCU would be no big deal?

Because as they finally reached their destination and Eve was about to meet the chief investigator of the OCU, Caine Valorian, a vampire, she realized it was a very big deal. She was scared…big-time. The fear was enough to make her want to pass out. When she stepped over the threshold of the tiny, stuffy office and came face-to-face with the most beautiful man that she had ever seen in her entire thirty years of life, she almost did.

She'd been expecting to see a man with long black hair, aristocratic features and pale blue eyes, like the haunting creatures described in most movies and books. Caine did have dark hair but it was cropped short around his ears, with the front a little longer and falling over his remarkably sculpted and handsome features. A little gray peppered the sides, giving him an air of distinction. His eyes were haunting, but they weren't pale. They were so blue she couldn't even put a name to the color. And he was tall. Tall enough to make her five-eight seem dwarfish in comparison. Looking at him, she imagined that she would fit quite nicely into the crook of his arm.

Oh Lord, she was in trouble. She had just arrived and she was already imagining the lead investigator on the case in flagrante.

Squeezing her lips together, she pasted on her very-nice-to-meet-you smile and offered her hand.

"It's an honor to meet you, Mr. Valorian. I'm Eve Grant. I've heard wonderful things about you and the work your team does here."

He took her offered hand with a look of amusement. "Nice to meet you, Eve." He glanced at the two bodyguards. "I didn't realize you were bringing your own assistants."

When he pulled his hand away, she noticed that he rubbed it on his pant leg. She wondered if it bothered him to touch her. She had heard about some Otherworlders' aversion to humans.

"Oh, no, these two don't belong to me." She started to smile when Caine smiled. "My Captain Morales thought it might be a good idea to have…ah, assistance into the city. Mr. Bask agreed."

"Of course he did," Caine remarked as he glanced at the baron. Eve could see the obvious distaste for the other vampire in his face.

"As I'm sure you realize, Caine, this situation is very sensitive and we thought, Lady Jannali and I, that it would be best if our guest here—" he nodded at Eve "—felt safe and secure in our city."

"Hmm, I see." Caine smiled at her again. "I'm sure Eve will feel quite safe here in the lab."

She cleared her throat, then nodded. "I do, thank you, Mr. Valorian."

"Caine, please."

"Caine." She nodded, although she had the sudden urge to lick her lips. "I think it would be best for everyone involved if we skipped the bodyguards."

"I couldn't agree more." Caine turned toward the baron. "Laal, if you could escort these gentlemen back to where they came from, I will make sure Eve is properly introduced to the team and informed on the status of the case."

Eve knew a dismissal when she heard one. She glanced at the baron and noticed that his eyes had got a lot brighter in the past few minutes. There was obviously some very bad blood between these two.

Thin-lipped and with a curt nod, Laal motioned to the two beefy men to follow him out of the office. He glanced at Eve on his way out. "I'll inform your captain of your cooperation."

When he was gone, Caine smiled again. Eve had to get herself together if she was going to work here. She had heard about the sexual potency of the male vampire, but no one had mentioned that the simple lifting of the lips alone could inflict feelings of instant desire. Although his lips were certainly full and sensuous, even soft-looking, she shouldn't be having daydreams about how they would feel on the sensitive spot under her ear. She would have to train herself to deal with his potency. But for now, she would just avoid eye contact.

"I apologize for the baron. He's a rather boorish man."

Chuckling, she waved her hand. "No need to apologize. I understand perfectly about politicians. We have them, too."

"Right, of course you do." He gestured toward the door. "Shall we meet the rest of the team?"

She nodded and followed him out. She tucked the stray hair behind her ear again. She wasn't sure if she was really ready to meet her new team. Before she came, she had read up on the members of the OCU. A couple of vampires, a couple of witches and a lycan. She wondered what else was on this team. A two-thousand-year-old mummy with bandages still hanging from its decaying body? She expected Bela Lugosi to jump out from around the corner any minute and say, "Good evening," in a thick Romanian accent.

Caine led her to a large, glassed-in room. The only one, she noticed, that didn't seem so cramped and stuffy, an obvious reminder that they were underground beneath the police station. Her own lab back in San Antonio was bright and cheerful, despite the fact that they dealt with violence and death every day.

There were three people in the room when they entered. One at the table eating, one lounging on a sofa with a huge textbook opened on her lap, and another with a tattooed bald head, tattooed arms and bright pale blue eyes, standing at the sink eating what looked like take-out Chinese.

They all stopped their various activities and stared at Eve when she walked in, still battling the hair coming loose from her hurriedly done French braid.

She knew she would be facing animosity when she volunteered for the job, but had no idea of the level of hostility until she entered the room. She could feel it physically, like a clammy fog floating over her when she stepped over the threshold. She found it difficult to breathe from the cloying thickness of it.

"Good, you're all here," Caine announced as he stepped back, allowing Eve to fully enter the room. "This is Eve Grant, from the San Antonio lab. She will be working with us on this case."

Eve smiled and tried to meet everyone's eyes. She managed to until she came to the tattooed man at the sink. He was grinning at her like a maniac. Pursing her lips, she nodded to him and then turned her attention back to Caine.

"I'll do the introductions, and then we'll get down to work." Gesturing to the petite dark-haired woman on the sofa, Caine said, "This is Lyra Magice. She specializes in spells, potions, poisons and healing." He nodded to the table. "Jace Jericho—bites, wounds, metals and audio and video analysis."

Eve nodded to them both, noticing that they both looked very normal. She'd never guess they were Otherworlders. Caine gestured to the man at the sink, noodles hanging out of his mouth.

"And this lunatic is Kellen Falcon. Specialties include explosives and ballistics."

Kellen slurped the last noodle into his mouth and grinned. "Chief, you forgot social director. I'm a frigging awesome party planner."

"Right." Caine smiled at Eve. "So, that's the team. You'll meet Gwen McKinley, she's in the lab, and Dr. Givon Silvanus in the morgue."

The one called Jace pushed up from the table, and tossed his paper plate into the garbage. "Welcome to the Boneyard," he barked. Making a wide path around her, he walked past without a smile and left the room.

Kellen approached her and rolled his eyes back into his sockets. "Welcome to the nuthouse." He stuck out his tongue and waggled it back and forth, his metal piercing flashing at her.

"Kel, go do something constructive," Caine chided.

He bowed his head and walked backward out of the room. "Yes, Master."

When he was gone, Caine turned to the woman still lounging on the sofa. Her head was buried in the thick volume of text on her lap. "Lyra, could you please get Eve up to speed on the case?"

"What? Why do I have to?" she whined.

Eve bristled inside. She knew why Caine had asked Lyra to be her guide. She was as close to human as an Otherworlder got, and the only other woman. A witch was essentially human, just with magical power and connections to other planes. Personally, Eve had never put much stock in witchcraft. Her best friend in high school had been a practicing Wiccan, and it didn't impress her much.

"Don't whine, Lyra. It's unbecoming for a witch of your station. What would your grandmother say?"

"She'd open a portal to another dimension and blast your butt through it, is what she'd say."

"Well, it's a good thing she's not working here and on my payroll, now is it?"

She stood and set her book down on the sofa. "Fine."

Caine smiled at Eve. "Lyra will also show you where you can put your things."

"Okay."

"Great." He nodded to her again, and then backed out of the room as if he couldn't leave fast enough. She had a feeling that Caine Valorian, despite his forced charm, wasn't too keen on her being here, either.

When he was gone, Eve looked at Lyra, who was

standing glaring at her from across the room. "So, um, where can I put my bag?"

The woman opened her mouth and it seemed to Eve that she was about to tell her exactly where she could put her bag. But she closed her mouth and walked toward Eve. "Follow me. I guess I'm your tour guide."

Eve followed her out of the staff room and back into the drab gray corridor. Lyra opened her arms wide and looked up toward the ceiling. "You see, Gran, this is why I think all men are sexist pigs."

Great, she'd been shackled with an insane person. What else could possibly go wrong? Eve pretended not to notice that the woman was conversing with thin air, until Lyra turned around and cocked her head as if deciding about something.

"Yeah, okay, I'll give her a chance."

"I'm sorry, were you talking to me?" Eve asked.

Lyra shook her head. "Gran says you're all right. That you have a part to play in all this."

"Oh, okay."

Eve lowered her gaze but kept walking. Maybe if she didn't keep eye contact, the woman would ignore her.

"But I told her she's crazy."

Eve smiled and nodded. *Right, her grandmother was crazy.*

Chapter 4

"I got you what you needed. Now when can I expect payment?"

The figure dressed in black stepped out of the shadows in the drawing room and into a soft pool of moonlight streaming in through the floor-to-ceiling window. His hooded cloak kept his face partially hidden. He spoke from beneath his hood, "Payment. Hmm, what exactly are you expecting?"

The vampire shifted in his seat, licking his lips. Fear floated off him like cheap cologne.

Oh, how the cloaked man hated vampires. Basically useless creatures. Vain and pompous, without reason. They had their purposes certainly, like the errand he had sent this particular one on. But he hated dealing with them, hated the fact that he *needed* them for his plans.

"Three hundred and fifty thousand. Cash." The vampire sat up straighter, trying to project confidence.

The cloaked man waved his hand in the air as if he was swatting away an insect. A big bald man dressed in black leather stepped toward the vampire and tossed a brown leather duffel bag onto his lap. The vampire squeezed the bag to his chest.

"Did you dispatch your accomplice?"

The vampire glanced up from inspecting the satchel and shook his head. "Not yet."

"Well, see that you do. I'm not pleased you included him in our operation. We can't have him walking around with information that can be used against me, now can we?"

"No. But I told you why I needed him. There was no way I could carry that much blood out by myself. Besides, he's my main source of V."

The shadowed figure sighed and waved his hand again. "Fine. Now get out. Our business is done."

The vampire rose and walked to the exit, hugging the bag to his chest. The burly guard opened the double doors and promptly ushered the vampire out, shutting them behind him.

"Do you trust him?" a voice spoke.

The cloaked man turned and glared at the source of the voice, into a corner where another form sat, unseen, shrouded in the dark.

"Of course I don't." He moved and sat in a burgundy leather chair near the fireplace, where a low fire still flickered. "That's why when he finishes his mission, he'll be taken care of like the rest."

"I heard the OCU has brought in someone from the outside to help with the case."

He smirked. "I'm not worried about Caine and his team of misfits." The police and crime lab didn't concern him; he'd been playing under their radar for a long time now without interference. There was no reason to suspect that that would change.

"They brought in a human to help with the case. A human woman."

Well, that did interest him. Sitting back in the chair, he chuckled. "Perfect."

Chapter 5

"So what's the new girl like?" Gwen asked as she poured liquid into the plastic test tube with the errant hair that Lyra had extracted from under the victim's fingernail.

Before Caine could respond, Jace growled from his perch beside Gwen. "She stinks."

"She does not, Jace," Caine protested.

"I can smell her a mile away. I know when someone stinks, and she does."

"Well, what does she smell like, then?" Gwen asked.

"Like plums and vanilla," Caine answered, not lifting his head from going over the other trace evidence they had logged. When it suddenly became as silent as a tomb, he glanced up. They were staring at him as if he had grown another head. This, of course, was genetically impossible. "What?"

"Ah, nothing, Chief." Jace smirked, then went back to filling test tubes with liquid.

"Is she pretty, then?"

Jace pushed off the worktable. "Who cares? She's an NOP."

Caine bristled. The last thing he needed was animosity within the team on this case. They couldn't afford to have biases blind them to the truth. "Jace, I'd appreciate if you didn't use that word in this lab. I will not tolerate any speciesism here."

"You hate them just as much as I do, Chief." Jace stared at Caine. "Hell, man, you have more reason than anyone here to hate them. What they did to you."

He put his hand up to stop any more accusations. "Although I find this matter as difficult to swallow as you do, I do not hate—"

"Excuse me?"

The soft, feminine sound came from the doorway. Caine swore under his breath and turned toward the voice. Eve stood framed in the doorway, her white-blond hair falling in her eyes. He wondered how long she had been listening to their conversation. He hoped not long.

However, by the look of anger and hurt on her face, he assumed she had been standing there long enough.

"Yes, Eve, hello. Has Lyra got you up to speed?" He walked toward her, hoping to defuse the situation.

"I need a computer." She brushed a stray hair

from her forehead and lifted her chin, but avoided meeting his eyes.

Caine had to admire her. She had likely heard everything they had said, and she still had the guts to walk in here and rise above the insults.

He'd been worried when he first saw her, looking like a Malibu Barbie doll. Long white-blond hair, dark blue eyes, blemish-free tanned skin, little pert nose with a sprinkling of freckles across the bridge. Thankfully, she was not rake thin. No, she definitely had curves. She filled out her navy pinstripe suit jacket and skirt very well. Not that he was trying to notice, it was just one of those things a man couldn't help but observe. For a human, he had to admit, she was attractive.

When he had taken her hand, he had felt something jolt through his skin. An energy of some sort. She wasn't psychic, but she possessed some kind of gift. And given the fact that his hand tingled after, remarkably with pleasure, she had certain sexual potency as well. Something, he believed, she had no idea that she possessed.

"Yes, of course," he answered, giving her his best diplomatic smile.

"I thought since the rest of the team is processing evidence, I would get a jump on IDing the victim. I can access AFIS, CODIS and missing persons reports."

"You have complete access to *all* the systems in San Antonio?"

Arching a brow, she smiled back at him. "What I don't have access to, I can hack."

Gwen whooped. "A girl after my own heart."

Caine's lips twitched. The woman had guts, he'd give her that. More than he expected from a human woman. Now, if she could back that up with skill, he'd be one happy crime investigator.

"You can use the computer in the analysis room." Still carrying his clipboard, Caine exited the lab and led the way down the hall to another small, enclosed area.

When he walked through the doorway of the analysis room, he stopped in his tracks, and Eve nearly collided with him. The computer was being used. Lyra was happily going through magical symbols and spells that she had archived in their system years ago.

Lyra glanced up at him and smiled smugly. "Why don't you let Eve use the computer in *your* office?"

Caine wanted to reach over and strangle Lyra. She knew how much he detested people being in his office, in his space. It wasn't that he was possessive about it. He just didn't like when others touched his things. Working as an OCI, he knew how germs could spread just by opening one's mouth.

"How long are you going to be?" he asked.

"As long as it takes to figure out these symbols, Chief." She raised her brow. "You do want me to figure that out, don't you?"

As Eve sidled up next to him curiously, he cleared his throat and nodded to Lyra, his little trouble-making witch, who he was tempted to write up under some insubordination charge. "Of course."

Turning toward Eve, he motioned toward the door. "We'll use my office."

Without a word, she followed him out and down the hall to his sanctuary.

Once through the door, he showed her where his computer was and motioned toward the chair for her to sit. Instead, she looked around his office, seeming to take everything in. She particularly eyed his book collection with intense scrutiny.

Before she could take a step toward his extensive and private collection of books, he moved in front of her blocking her path. He motioned toward the computer once again.

"Do you need some help getting started?"

He meant the question to be condescending, and by the dark gleam in her eye, he suspected he made his point.

Lifting one perfect brow, Eve flexed her fingers and sat down in his chair in front of the computer. "No. I think I can handle it, thank you."

Caine watched, at first unconcerned and then with rising interest, as her fingers flew over the keyboard accessing more programs and screens than he'd ever seen. In five minutes, she had full access to the San Antonio police department mainframe and was tapping into AFIS and CODIS. Using the prints and DNA samples they had on the victim, she ran both searches at once.

Seemingly very satisfied with herself, Eve leaned back in his chair and smiled up at him, the blue in her eyes sparkling. "May take awhile, but at least we're in. If she's in the system, we'll find her."

"Great." He nodded. "You're, ah, very efficient with the computer."

"Thank you. I've been hacking systems since I could type. This was when I was four." She laughed.

He joined in, intrigued by the dimple in her right cheek and the crinkle of her eyes. She didn't look like a Barbie doll right then, more like a confident woman. A warm tingling radiated up his spine, telling him he needed to get out of this situation. The room suddenly became too small, too warm. She was too close. Taking a distancing step back, he rubbed a hand over his face.

"It's my shampoo, by the way."

He looked at her, eyebrow lifted in question.

"Plums and vanilla." She touched her hair with the tips of her fingers. "That's what you smell."

Before he could comment, his cell phone buzzed. Feeling very aware of Eve's presence, Caine turned from her amused gaze and flipped open his phone. "Valorian."

While Mahina grumbled in his ear, Caine felt Eve watching him. He sensed that she was eyeing him up and down, taking in everything about him. Glancing over his shoulder, he watched her face blush and she quickly turned her head, her attention focusing back on the computer screen.

He needed to get out of the office, and now. It was becoming excessively uncomfortable in here. Thank the moon, Mahina needed him at the crime scene.

He flipped his phone closed, pocketed it and shuffled his clipboard from one hand to the other. Without looking at Eve, he started toward the door. "I need to go back to the crime scene, so if you'll excuse—"

"Can I come?"

Pausing, his foot just over the threshold, Caine turned around. "I'm sorry?"

"The search will take awhile. I could sit here in your office and paw through your things, or you could take me with you to the crime scene."

Again, that sparkle in the blue of her eyes flashed at him. She could read that he didn't want her in his office around his personal effects.

Sighing, he nodded.

With a smile, she stood, smoothed down the line of her skirt and followed him out.

The intoxicating scent of plums and vanilla clung to her like a gossamer spiderweb.

He had no desire to be the fly lured into it.

Chapter 6

It was nearing ten in the evening when Caine maneuvered the lab's black SUV into the Black Heart Hotel's parking lot. Eve had stared out the passenger window as they whizzed through the city, taking in everything she could.

Necropolis wasn't all that different from any other city in America.

High-rises brushed the night sky. Storefronts lined the busy streets. Fluorescent signs declared this week's special sales. Couples out on the town lined up to get into the hottest nightclubs. *What were you expecting? Neon signs flashing: Beware Vampires Live Here?*

She'd seen all the same things in San Antonio, and

it was easy to forget that these people were not the same. They were *Other.* And *she* was the outsider.

Glancing over at Caine, she thought the same about him. He was nothing like she'd expected him to be. Vampires were supposed to be flamboyant and extravagant, with a penchant for flair and dramatics, just like in the movies. But Caine was the exact opposite of that. He seemed aloof and reserved. Right down to his cornflower-blue tie and pressed gray slacks. At first, he had been charming, with his killer smile, but now he seemed almost nervous. Why would he be nervous around her? It's not like he had anything to fear from her.

Opening the passenger door, the heat of the sultry night hit her full blast. It was hot in the summer in Texas, but lately it had been unbearably humid as well. Already, her blouse was sticking to her back as she rounded the vehicle and grabbed her field kit from the back.

Caine had offered her one of theirs, but she had come to Necropolis with her own stainless-steel, fully packed kit. Everything was right where she needed it. Using someone else's gear just didn't feel right to her. Like wearing someone else's clothes.

With her kit in hand, she followed Caine into the hotel.

"This is the Black Heart. One of a few unsavory hotels here in the Digs."

She glanced around the lobby, taking in the grime on the yellowing linoleum floor and the greasy sheen on the walls. Definitely not the Four Seasons.

They took the stairs up to the second floor. Eve was very careful not to touch the railing. She didn't like the look of the substances stuck on the flaking orange-painted metal. One she was certain was gum, but the other goo she really didn't even want to think about. Her stomach was already queasy as it was.

This was technically her first crime scene. Back in San Antonio, she had worked the lab. For two years, she processed evidence and maintained the computer lab. When she was training, she'd been out on a few crime scenes, but this was the first time she was out here by herself, or without anyone she knew, that is. She really hoped she didn't blow it. Captain Morales had given her the opportunity for this assignment, and she didn't want to disappoint him. Because she knew if she failed out here, she would never get another chance to prove herself.

When they arrived on the second floor, Eve noticed a muscular woman in jeans and T-shirt standing with a scrawny weasel of a man and a taller man in a suit in front of an open doorway with yellow tape across it. The crime scene.

Caine nodded to the woman. "Mahina."

"Valorian." She turned her scrutiny onto Eve. "Who's this?"

"This is Eve Grant from the San Antonio lab. She's helping with the case."

Mahina smiled. The woman's grin made Eve's stomach clench. She swore the woman was eyeing her as if she were a late-night snack.

"Eve, this is Captain Mahina Garner."

Mahina stuck out her hand. Eve took it reluctantly. "Nice to meet you."

Eve had to stifle a gasp as the police captain almost crushed her hand. Finally, she let go, and Eve nearly sighed in relief. "You, too."

The man in the suit grunted. "Can we move on to my problem, please?"

Caine turned his attention to the man. Eve could see a slight rise in the way Caine stood, a shifting of his shoulders, a tilting of his chin. A predatory stance? She supposed she shouldn't be surprised by it. Males of any species showed aggression when confronted by another male. It was natural. However, for some reason, she really seemed to notice it in him.

"And what is the issue, Mr. Porter?"

"I'm losing money keeping this room quarantined."

Eve glanced sideways and looked into room 210. She was itching to get inside and look around. She imagined Caine's team had done a thorough job of collecting the evidence, but sometimes fresh—even foreign—eyes could pick out things that they couldn't see.

She tapped Caine on the arm and motioned to the room. "May I?"

He nodded briefly. "Just look, don't touch." Dismissively, he then turned his attention back to the uptight man in the suit, the hotel's owner, she assumed.

"Mr. Porter, this room is a crime scene, and it will continue to be blocked off until we are satisfied that we've collected all the evidence we need to solve this case."

Eve opened her kit, snapped on a pair of latex gloves and wandered into the room, leaving the men to argue. She took small measured steps on a straight path, trying to note every detail: The way the room was arranged, the smell of disinfectant and the sharp metallic odor of blood. She set her kit down on the floor and neared the bed.

Back at the lab, she had looked over the crime-scene photos briefly. But she remembered the way the girl looked sprawled out on the bed, as if she were viewing it right now. The grisly image had been ingrained in her memory. The way her arms were splayed out to the sides, and her legs spread. To Eve she had looked like a five-pointed star positioned like that. A pentagram, Eve had thought. The symbols written on the girl's bare chest and stomach had been foreign to Eve. She'd never seen anything like it. However, she didn't need to be a witch to comprehend that the girl had been an unwilling part of a spell or sacrifice of some sort.

Why and how had the girl come here? Where would she have met a vampire?

For the most part, the existence of the Otherworld community was a guarded secret from the rest of humanity. Because of its proximity to San Antonio, some people knew of the undead city and its inhabitants. Those in law enforcement had been made aware, and each of them had to sign a contract that kept their silence and prevented them from speaking about the Others to anyone. If that silence was broken, the perpetrator was severely dealt with.

Eve had signed such a contract when she was hired as a forensic investigator. There had been lots of speculation on what the otherworlders were like, lots of misinformation and prejudice. She had read the files on each of the species, on each of the OCU members, but it didn't prepare her at all for the reality of the situation. She was as ignorant about them here as she was before.

So, how did this young, seemingly innocent girl hook up with a killer vampire? Maybe she had been kidnapped or seduced by his vampiric charms. But if that had been the case, then the vampire had been in San Antonio.

On a hunting trip.

That thought brought shivers over Eve's body. Shaking her head from her dangerous thoughts, Eve turned from the bed, intent on leaving, and nearly collided with the weasel-like man from the hallway.

He was grinning at her. "Do you need some help?"

Immediately, her heart started to thump in her chest. All kinds of warning bells sounded in her head. "Um, you shouldn't be in here. This is a crime scene."

"I know," he sniveled, then wiped his mouth with his hand. Had there been drool slicking his thin lips?

Eve distanced herself from him and tried to remain calm. "Would you please leave the room?"

He moved toward her. "You smell good, human."

Eve took a step back, right into her field kit. Two seconds later, she was falling backward. When she landed flat on her back, the little scrawny vampire loomed over her, licking his lips. He grinned, showing his fangs. Saliva dribbled from his open mouth and down his pointy chin.

Scrambling for anything to protect herself, Eve grabbed the ALS flashlight fastened to her belt. She unhooked it and bashed it across the vampire's head. The impact of the hard plastic didn't even make him flinch. He continued to press down on her, baring his elongated teeth. She flicked on the light and flashed it in his eyes. Ultraviolet in the face had to hurt. The vampire shrieked and closed his eyes but continued to close in on her. She opened her mouth and screamed.

Faster than she could see, the little man was lifted off the ground. Caine stood above her, his hand wrapped tightly around the weasel man's throat. The vampire's shoes didn't reach the ground as he dangled there, held up by Caine's pure brute strength.

"I could crush you like a cockroach." Caine's voice was hard and cold. Eve had to suppress a violent shiver, as the room's temperature seemed to drop rapidly.

Mahina moved around to Caine's side, an amused look on her face. "Hey, Valorian, put the little bloodsucker down before he pisses in his pants and ruins your crime scene and your three-hundred-dollar shoes."

Eve watched as the feral look on Caine's face faded. She could see him start to relax, letting his shoulders droop. Slowly, he set the weasel down, and then took a step back, his breathing labored but slowing. The room seemed to warm at the same rate as his breathing slowed.

"Take him in," Caine demanded.

Mahina raised her eyebrow, but said nothing. She took hold of the little vampire's arm and dragged him toward the door. "Okay, Chuck, we're taking a ride."

"But I didn't do anything!" Chuck sputtered.

Once they were through the door, Caine turned and looked down at Eve. His face seemed to soften as he eyed her. "Are you okay?"

Sighing, Eve closed her eyes. She let her body relax on the carpet. Relief surged over her. For a moment there, she thought she was going to die. Slowly opening her eyes, she swallowed down the residual panic. Then she paused, spying something foreign under the bed.

Craning her neck, she squinted and tried to make out the shape lying on the carpet a few feet away.

Caine reached down and grabbed her arm. "Here let me help you."

Eve pulled away from his grip and rolled onto her stomach. "Get me some tweezers and a plastic bag will you?"

"Excuse me?"

She glanced at Caine and raised an eyebrow. "An evidence bag, please."

He took her case, opened it, grabbed a pair of long tweezers and a bag and handed it to her. Taking them, Eve shuffled on her belly toward the bed and reached as far as she could underneath. Carefully, she plucked the white object from the shag carpet, shuffled backward and rolled over into a sit, bringing the object up into view.

It was about two inches long, blanched and sharpened into a point. She'd seen one before on several occasions, but never like this. Usually, they were attached to the rest of the skeleton.

"It's a phalange," Caine announced.

Smiling, Eve bagged the bone and sealed the sack shut. "Good thing I was attacked and ended up on the floor. We might have missed that."

Caine offered her his hand. This time she took it and allowed him to pull her to her feet. Still holding her hand in his, he remarked, "Interesting tactics, but good work."

She gave him a little smile, but pulled her hand from his. Heat had suddenly enveloped her, and she didn't want to even consider where it was coming from. She took a step back, and reached for her kit to stash the evidence she'd retrieved.

Caine cleared his throat. "I shouldn't have left you alone. I wasn't thinking."

"It's all right. I wouldn't have seen the bone if I hadn't been on the floor."

"It should never have happened, Eve. I have to remember that you are not…Other. Leaving you alone is dangerous, negligent even, and I won't do it again."

She waved his apology away. "I don't need a babysitter. I'm fine. I can take care of myself, you know. I have training."

"Not for Necropolis, you don't."

With that, she noticed his eyes flashed like blue flames, reminding her that she was indeed an outsider in a foreign place with unfamiliar people. People that could kill her in a blink of an eye. Even Caine possessed that power.

Her stomach clenched again, and she had to fight the rising panic of being here, in this place of strangeness, with a vampire. Once a creature of myth, but certainly now as real as she was. Maybe she wasn't completely prepared, but she refused to be scared away. She refused to back down from this challenge. She was here until the end, whether she, or Caine, liked it or not.

Squaring her shoulders, she picked up her kit. "I'm fine. Now, let's get back to the lab and figure out this puzzle piece."

With that, she brushed past Caine and walked toward the door. The fact that her wobbling knees still supported her and she was able to walk without passing out surprised her to no end. Just as it probably surprised Caine when she felt him following close behind.

Chapter 7

Blood spotted the stone steps of the dais.

The cloaked figure in the shadows watched as his servants prepared the sacrificial altar, splashing the human's blood over the gray consecrated stone. His body thrummed with excited anticipation of the events to come. It wouldn't be long before his purpose was fulfilled and he could finally go home.

He'd come to Necropolis years ago, quickly adapting to the city and integrating himself into the Otherworld society. He worked and played just like everyone else. No one had any clue of his true purpose, or his true identity. He had successfully fooled everyone into thinking that he was one of them. Little did they know how wrong they truly were.

One of the servants, an eager young witch, scurried over to where he waited, shrouded in the dark. She bowed to him. "Everything is just as you instructed, Master."

"Good." He touched the top of her head. "Soon you will be rewarded for your dedication."

She bowed again, even lower. "Thank you, Master." Then she scurried away to finish the last of her tasks.

So eager his servants were to please him. Willing to do anything he asked of them. And he had asked many things. Others he had paid to do his bidding— like the vampire that had acquired the human woman's blood—and he'd paid well. Money meant nothing to him. He had plenty of it and it was for this purpose only. After the ceremony took place, he'd have no need for money, or anything else he could acquire in this world.

Everything he ever wanted, ever desired, lay within his reach. Soon, he would have more power than any amount of money could buy.

Soon, the world—human and Otherworlder alike—would bow to him.

Chapter 8

"It's not vampire, lycan or human."

Caine frowned at Givon, as he inspected the bone they had found at the crime scene. Givon had it under his magnifying glass.

"An ape, then?" Eve piped up from her perch beside Caine.

Givon shook his head. "I'm not an expert, but I'd say not." He pointed to the bone. "If this is a distal phalanx bone, which I'm sure it is, it's way too short to be human or ape."

Impatience thumped at Caine's head, giving him the beginnings of a killer headache. "What then? Some other animal?"

"I don't know." Givon lifted his glasses and rubbed

his fingers over the bridge of his nose. Caine knew his friend well, and was familiar with the subtle nuances of Givon's body language. Fiddling with his glasses screamed aggravation at not knowing answers.

Sighing, Caine ran his hand through his own hair. He had been hoping for a break, something, anything that would lead them somewhere on this case. So far, they had nothing.

No hits on the Otherworld DNA or fingerprint catalogues. Nothing on the human ones, either. He was hoping the bone would lead them to the next clue, then to the next, like a treasure hunt. Nothing. They were on this hunt without a map to guide them.

"Do we know any anthropologists?" Caine asked.

Givon nodded. "I know a guy who might help us. A civilian, though."

"Call him, Givon. We need something."

The door to the morgue opened, and Jace peeked his head in. "We got a hit."

Minutes later, the whole team gathered in Caine's office while Eve pulled up the results of her search. The vic's prints showed up in the system from a prior arrest, a drunk and disorderly.

"Lillian Ann Crawford, twenty years old." Eve read off the screen. "86 Soleada Way, San Antonio."

Caine wanted to feel some relief that they had identified their victim, but instead a sense of melancholy washed over him. As he looked around at his team, he could see the same sadness on their collective faces, except maybe Kellen's. He never seemed fazed by the crimes.

They had a name, which was a good thing, but somehow that seemed to make it more real. Death was always sad, but when it happened to someone so young, Caine felt a sense of loss creep over him.

Shaking off the feeling, Caine addressed Eve. "We need to talk to her family and friends. Someone knows how this girl ended up in a motel room with a vampire."

"I'll call Captain Morales." Eve picked up the phone on Caine's desk.

As she dialed, Caine motioned to the rest of his team to follow him out into the hallway. Once assembled, he looked at each of them.

"Someone needs to go with Eve into San Antonio to talk with the family. The right questions need to be asked, and I have no faith in the human police to ask them."

Lyra sniffed. "Don't look at me. I still have those symbols to decipher. I think I'm really close."

Caine moved his gaze to Jace. The man's face was so stern, his eyes so fierce, that Caine didn't even bother to ask.

Kellen raised his hand. "I'll go with her." He grinned. "She's just the type of distraction I need."

"Not likely, Kel. You're a lab man, not a field man. You'd scare the residents of San Antonio." Sighing, Caine shook his head. "Save it. I'll go. You're all acting like juveniles out on the playground."

Jace snorted. "Hey, you're the boss. You're the one

that's supposed to be the professional and set an example for the rest of us."

"You had better have made some progress on the hair and fiber analysis when I get back," Caine remarked, then marched back into his office.

Eve had just hung up the phone and glanced at him as he neared the desk. She looked harried, strands of hair framing her face. He noticed that she didn't try to tuck them back behind her ears. Obviously, she was too preoccupied to worry about it. A slight twitch at her right cheek beside her lips indicated nervous tension. He could just imagine what her captain had said to her about one of them coming into San Antonio to question some humans.

"He's sending someone to meet us at the east entrance." She lowered her gaze, and tapped a finger on his desk. "They'll escort us to the Crawford residence where Detective Salinas will meet us."

He nodded. He hadn't expected anything less. He was actually surprised that they were allowing any of them to enter San Antonio. It had been over ten years since he'd been in the city.

"I'm surprised." He lifted his brow with an unasked question.

"I told the captain that the case couldn't possibly be solved without you…without your questions, I mean—" she cleared her throat "—that only an Otherworlder would be able to ask the right questions to get the answers we need to solve Lillian's murder."

"What's this Detective Salinas like? Do you know him?"

She nodded but refused to meet his gaze. Was she hiding something? "He's all right. Fairly straight up."

Caine stiffened. Was that hurt he heard in her voice? Possibly anger? He wasn't as sensitive to sound as Jace, but he could decipher a lot in the way people spoke, and the words they used to communicate. He had extraordinary sensory perception. And right now, it was telling him that there was obviously some history between Eve and Detective Salinas. Romantic history, he assumed by the way her cheeks turned pink when she spoke about him.

"Is there going to be a problem working with him? Is your past history going to interfere with this investigation?"

Her head snapped up and the color of her eyes darkened. It was obvious he had hit a nerve. "What do you mean?"

"Well, I'm assuming you've had some sort of relationship with the detective. Is it going to be an issue working with him? We can't afford any more liabilities on this case."

Standing, Eve straightened her shoulders and glared at him. "First of all, it's none of your business if I've had a relationship with this man or not. You are not my boss, thank God for that." She rounded the desk and stood directly in front of him, her hands on her hips. He could feel her anger float off her like heat waves. He could almost taste it in the air on the tip of his tongue. "Secondly, I am *not* a liability. The biggest problem with this case is the hostility here. I sense it with your team—and now with you."

Without waiting for him to comment, she stormed out of his office.

That went well. Caine rubbed a hand over his mouth. He supposed he deserved that for assuming any impropriety on Eve's part. It was just that they didn't need any more problems on this case. He didn't believe in engaging in anything romantic with coworkers. Nothing good ever came out of it. It was difficult enough without making things more complicated with strained working relationships.

Ha! Talk about strained working relationships! Just having Eve here had put enough tension on his team, and on him, to break a tightrope. He could feel the high level of anxiety from both his people and from Eve. It was so palpable he felt like he was walking in quicksand.

Jace popped his head through the doorway. "What did you do to the human? She looks like she could rip the universe a new black hole...with her teeth even."

"I probably owe her an apology." He sighed. "Did you happen to see where she went?"

"Women's washroom. I heard some definite banging going on in there." As quick as Jace was there, he was gone.

Taking a deep breath, Caine smoothed a hand over his hair, then exited his office and walked down the hall toward the washrooms.

He put his ear to the door, and heard some mumbling. The word *jerk* and a few choice swear words came through a little louder than normal. Yup, she was definitely in there.

Without announcing his intentions, Caine pushed open the door and walked in. Eve was leaning on the counter, her head down, with the tap running. There were a few balled-up wads of tissue paper lined up on the Formica near her fisted hand.

She glanced up when he walked in. Fumbling for the tap, she turned off the water, and then gathered all her tissues and shoved them into the garbage can.

"What are you doing in here? This isn't a coed facility, is it?" She looked around, obviously searching for any missed urinals.

"I wanted to apologize." He cleared his throat, and smoothed a hand over his shirt, pressing down on a wrinkle he just noticed. "You're right that it is none of my business in how you handle your…affairs, and I'm sure, if handled properly, that it wouldn't interfere with this investigation in any way."

When he was done, he noticed that she was staring at him, her brow wrinkled as if in deep thought.

"Do all your apologies sound so forced and contrived?"

"If by that, you mean I'm not used to apologizing, then you'd be correct. I suppose I'm not used to someone so emotional that I would need to make an apology."

Shaking her head, Eve turned back to the sink, turned on the tap and started to wash her hands. "You come in here all intent on apologizing to me, and end up insulting me again." She sniffed. "Go figure."

Caine blew out a breath, and then tried again. He wasn't used to having to coddle anyone. Everyone on his team did his or her job without complaint. He'd had to discipline both Lyra and Jace several times on their behavior, but neither one had displayed any emotion other than anger. He wasn't used to having to explain himself or his behavior. It was uncomfortable and he didn't like it much.

"Eve, we are very different. The way we work, the way we think, and the obvious physical differences." He took in a deep breath, trying to sort through his thoughts so they came out coherently. "I will try and remember that so I think before I speak to you."

She glanced at him sideways, then nodded. Turning, she wiped her hands on a paper towel and gave him a half smile. "I accept your apology."

"And for the record, when I was talking about liabilities, I was in no way referring to you."

She gave him a genuine smile, and her face lit up. He thought she looked quite beautiful, even with her hair in disarray. In fact, he preferred her that way. Unkempt, fresh faced and…stunning.

Clearing his throat again, he looked away and fiddled with a button on his shirt. Where these sudden nerves came from, he didn't know. He was usually wound tight, confident, unfazed. However, being around this human, with her looking at him the way she was, started to unravel some of his tight threads. And he didn't like the feeling one bit.

"And I'm sorry for calling you and your team hostile," she said as she tucked her hair behind her ear.

He shook his head. "No need. We are. However, we need to all get along and try to work as a team. I know you are trying." He smiled at her. "I know we seem like a freak show to you, and I appreciate your professionalism in not letting it get to you."

She smiled at him gently, and for a moment it was as if the room had disappeared, as if it was just the two of them standing across from one another in an empty white space. Caine felt an intense connection between them. A connection he hadn't experienced in a very long time.

However, as soon as the moment came, it disappeared.

"We have to leave soon." He turned toward the door. "Why don't you get something to eat, and I'll meet you in the garage."

He left before she could say anything. The moment he was out of the washroom, he took in a deep cleansing breath and rubbed at his eyes. This was going to be one hell of a case, and it had nothing to do with the murder.

Squeezing his hands into fists, he pushed down the hunger coursing through his body. This was not the time or place for his sexual appetites to be rising to the surface. He was close to three-hundred years old, for pity's sake, and had long ago learned how to control his urges. He had stopped frequenting the Club, hadn't he, since gaining control over himself? No longer feeling the need for the tension-relieving facilities to regulate his desires, he had revoked his membership.

However, there was something about the woman that battered at his senses. Something that yanked the bars on his cage. If he wasn't careful, those metal bars around his desire would dissolve into molten steel and no one would be safe. Especially not a defenseless human woman like Eve.

Chapter 9

By the time they drove out of Necropolis and onto I-35 toward San Antonio, the silence was killing Eve. She was normally a quiet, introspective person, but sitting in the same vehicle as Caine, with his spicy cologne tickling her senses, was stretching her nerves. It was becoming increasingly difficult to stay still and pensive.

She had busied herself looking out the passenger window as they drove down the dark road, but there were only so many road signs that could occupy a person's mind. There was nothing to see out in the darkened desert. The only thing she could discern were the lights of San Antonio as they approached.

His presence was starting to affect her. Oh, she'd

been careful to avoid eye contact with him—at least as much as was possible, given they worked together, but she found she enjoyed being around him. Although he was uptight, arrogant and seemingly very anal about his office and personal things, she was starting to like him.

It was obvious to her that his crime investigation team and the law enforcement community respected him. He ran a tight unit and she had been impressed with what he had done with the lab. She'd heard from Lyra that Caine had created most of the systems and procedures. When Necropolis was formed, and its citizens were given their own level of government and law, Caine was the one who oversaw the creation of the OCU, without much help from the human community.

She respected that level of dedication and determination. But she supposed having lived so long allowed him time to become goal driven.

After fiddling with the glove box, Eve glanced over at Caine. His eyes were straight forward, his hands tight on the wheel, and he looked very focused on driving. Focused. That was a good way to describe him. She wondered if he attacked every task, every activity, with such concentration.

For a brief moment, an image of Caine flashed in her mind. Sexy and sleek, he stalked across a room toward her, his gorgeous blue eyes glinting like cobalt blue steel.

She shook her head, dislodging the image, and turned back to the glove box. *Keep your mind on the boring gray plastic. Much safer that way.*

"Would you like some music?"

She nodded, eager for anything to break the disturbing tension the sexual images created in her.

Caine turned on the SUV's stereo system. Within seconds, the hauntingly melodious sound of stringed instruments floated through the speakers. Eve thought she had never heard anything so breathtaking in her life. At least, not until the poignant heart-wrenching voice joined in. Instantly, tears sprang to her eyes and her chest tightened with emotion. She could hardly breathe; the intensity felt like it was crushing her.

"Oh my God," she said, wiping her eyes with the back of her hand. "I have never heard anything so beautiful, so moving."

"Nadja Devanshi." Caine sighed. "She sings like an angel."

The tears flowed freely down her face and she closed her eyes while listening to the music. It was an opera, she was sure, but it was sung in a language she'd never heard before. However, she didn't need to understand the words to know that the song was about loss and pain. Eve could feel it in her heart, in her head. Nothing like this had ever affected her before. It seemed almost unnatural.

Her eyes sprang open and she looked at Caine. "Turn it off."

"What?"

"I said turn it off. Please."

He pushed the stop button on the stereo. Abruptly, they were plunged into silence. "What's the matter?"

"Her voice. It seemed to overpower me."

Caine shook his head. "Right. I should've known. I didn't realize it would affect you so intensely."

Eve ran a hand over her face, scrubbing away the last of her tears. The tightness in her chest lessened, and she was able to breathe without feeling the need to sob uncontrollably.

"Do you have that…that power?" she asked, her voice quiet, the need to cry still clutching at her throat.

"No. Every vampire is different."

"Does her voice affect you?"

He chuckled. "Yes, I suppose it does, but not in the same way it did you."

"What is your power?"

"I can sense things, strong emotions mostly." He glanced at her. "If someone is afraid, even if they try to mask it, I can sense their fear." He turned his gaze back to the dark road. "It comes to me as a smell or taste."

"All emotions?"

He nodded, and she thought she saw a twitch of his lips. "Some more than most."

She stared at his profile, wanting to trace a fingertip along the line of his jaw. His muscles twitched there, and for some reason, she wanted to smooth it away. She wondered if he could sense that she wanted to touch him, if he could smell her blossoming attraction.

Pulling her gaze from him, she looked down at her hands and tried to will her feelings away. Just knowing that he could sense them, taste them even, made her even more uncomfortable than before. It was hard enough keeping them from her face, or from her voice. To know that Caine could read them anyway, no matter what she did, caused a treacherous ripple of pleasure over her body. She shivered, knowing that he could probably read that, too.

"Are you cold?" he asked while he turned on the heater.

She nodded, relieved that he attributed her quivers to the temperature. However, the gleam in his eye as he turned his gaze to the SUV's controls, told her he knew damn well what caused the goose bumps on her arms and legs. And it wasn't the lack of warmth in the vehicle, but the rising heat in her body.

He flicked on the heat hoping to lessen the tension in the vehicle. Tension that was quickly becoming sexual more than anything else. Caine could smell Eve's increasing attraction toward him. Not the way most males could by the scent of her body, it was something more. Something floral, sweet and enticing. An odor he didn't want to discern. Because her attraction to him only increased his toward her.

Tightening his hold on the steering wheel, Caine directed his thoughts away from the beautiful woman sitting beside him to more pressing matters: the case.

It was starting to unnerve him that they had so few clues. No crime was perfect. It was impossible for a murderer to exact his force on another without leaving pieces of himself behind. But so far, the team had nothing concrete that was pointing them in any one direction.

He knew eventually it would come together; it always did. Criminals didn't remain free for long. Not in his city, anyway. Something always gave them away. He just hoped that they could find that something soon. If this case remained unsolved, the scrutiny on Necropolis and its inhabitants would steadily rise.

It wouldn't be long before the humans took matters into their own hands. He'd seen it before, so many times before. War, bloodshed, persecution. The Otherworlders had already been rounded up and tagged. Watched constantly. It wouldn't take much more for that to increase. Soon, there would be electronic surveillance or worse.

He would do what he had to, to make sure that never happened.

Solving this case was what mattered. For more reasons than just catching a criminal. It was about the survival of his people. If they didn't find out something soon, he feared the worst.

Chapter 10

When they arrived at the victim's place of residence, Caine noticed two cop cars and an unmarked sedan parked in front. For a moment, he wondered if there had been another crime committed, but then he realized they were there because of him. He parked on the opposite side of the street, their escort parking behind him.

After he jumped out of the SUV, he went around back and opened the hatch so he and Eve could grab their kits. Once equipped, they walked up the cement walkway to the front door of the blue trimmed two-story house. A uniformed officer greeted them on the porch.

He glared at Caine, and then turned his gaze to

Eve and nodded. "They're waiting for you in the living room." He opened the door for them.

Caine motioned for Eve to go first. It would be best if the victim's family and Detective Salinas saw her first. Maybe it would cut down on the animosity he could sense all around him.

Upon entering the house, Caine took note of the simple furnishings and decorations. Simple and understated, like a picture from *Better Homes and Gardens.* It was obvious the Crawford family was solvent. Not wealthy by any means, but comfortable.

As he followed Eve through the entranceway and into a large, homey room, Caine noticed a few family photos on the walls. Mom, dad, Lillian and a younger male sibling. All smiling. One average happy family.

When they entered the living room, a large man with a shirt and tie stood up. His eyes took in Eve, a quick assessment, and then locked on to Caine. Caine could feel the man's hate as if someone had poured hot water on his head.

Detective Salinas looked like a man made of iron. Wide shoulders, barrel chest and big meaty hands that now clenched at his sides. Caine was strong, stronger than any human, but he would've thought twice about tangoing with the steely-eyed cop.

Eve took a step forward, blocking the detective's line of vision. "Aaron."

He nodded to her. "Eve. Good to see you."

"You, too." She glanced over her shoulder. "This is Caine Valorian from the other lab."

Caine tipped his head. "Detective Salinas."

Aaron ignored him and motioned toward the couple sitting on the pale blue sofa. "John and Barbara Crawford."

Eve nodded to them respectfully. "Sir. Ma'am."

Caine observed that the couple sat apart on the sofa, indicating a level of guilt and accusation between them. He wondered who blamed whom for Lillian's rebellion and eventual disappearance.

"Do you have news about our daughter?" Barbara asked, her hands wringing in her lap.

Eve looked at Caine. He nodded his head to indicate for her to proceed. It was best that everything came from her. No one would appreciate his input. Not now. Not when the girl's slaying was so fresh in their minds.

Setting her kit down, Eve slid out some autopsy photos of Lillian from the manila envelope she'd been carrying under her arm. She set one of the photos, a facial shot, on the coffee table in front of the Crawfords.

"Is this your daughter Lillian?"

They both looked down at the black-and-white photo of the dead girl's face. By the wave of horror that surged over him, Caine had no doubt that they recognized the dead girl to be their daughter, Lillian Crawford. He could taste their anguish in the air. It was bitter.

Barbara covered her face in her hands and sobbed. The father just stared down at the photo, unmoving, his hands curled over his knees like claws.

"How did she die? Can we see her?"

Eve picked up the photo from the table and slid

it back into the envelope. "She was murdered, sir, out of town."

He looked up at her then, and even from across the room, Caine could see the pain in the man's eyes. Caine had no doubt that neither parent was involved in the girl's death. They may have pushed her away, or misunderstood her, but they didn't contribute to her actual murder.

Barbara's sobbing increased. John looked at her. Caine thought he was going to say something. Instead, with a shaking hand, he reached out and touched her shoulder. Turning, she threw herself into his arms, burying her face into the safety of his shoulder. He wrapped his arms around her tightly, tears now streaming down his cheeks.

"Who did this to our girl?" John choked out.

"We're working on that, sir," Detective Salinas grunted. "But I promise you this, we will do *every-thing* possible to find her killer. You have my word on this." His hardened gaze turned to Caine.

Caine kept Detective Salinas's gaze, his predatory instincts rising to the surface. He would only allow the man so much leeway with his prejudice and hate before it crossed the line. If the cop pushed him too hard, he'd push back, and it wouldn't be pretty.

Eve cleared her throat, jostling both men back to the task at hand, and addressed the Crawfords. "We need to ask you some questions to help us in our investigation. Would that be all right?"

Mr. Crawford nodded, letting go of his wife and wiping his eyes.

"Lillian lived here with you?"

"Yes. She was planning to move out next year with—" he paused "—a friend."

"A boyfriend?" Eve interjected.

He nodded.

"What's his name?" Detective Salinas asked, his pen poised over his small pocket notebook.

"Chad Murphy."

"Do you have his phone number or address?"

He nodded.

"Was it usual for your daughter to be out all night, or gone for days?" Eve asked.

Mr. Crawford nodded again. "We were starting to worry about the people she was hanging around with. Strange bunch of kids."

Caine stepped forward. "Strange…how?"

"They wore black all the time even when it was ninety degrees. Black and white makeup, red lipstick. Even the boys." He ran a hand over his face. "Dressed like, like what's the style called?" He glanced up at Eve.

"Goth?"

"Yeah, that's it. Goth." He shook his head. "They all looked like damn vampires to me."

Eve and Detective Salinas swiveled and stared at Caine. He didn't meet either of their gazes and looked straight at Mr. Crawford. "Can we search your daughter's room?"

He motioned toward the hallway to the right of the living room. "The last room on your right."

"Thank you." Caine snapped on a pair of latex

gloves, then proceeded to move toward the hallway. Eve followed him, also putting on a pair of gloves.

"I'm sorry about Aaron," she said softly as they reached the last door on the right.

Caine wrapped his hand around the doorknob and turned, pushing the door open. "Don't worry about it. It's not your fault he's an asshole, is it?"

"No, I blame his parents."

The moment Caine crossed the threshold of the girl's room, he began scanning the room, looking for anything that would give them a clue as to how Lillian Crawford ended up with a vampire's fangs in her neck.

Her bed was neatly made. The things on her dresser and desk were precisely arranged. The girl was orderly and tidy. There were no clothes tossed on the floor or shoes lying haphazardly on the rug. No outward signs yet on how she ended up with the wrong crowd.

Eve made her way toward the girl's desk. A pink-colored laptop sat open on the bleached oak frame. "I'll check her computer."

While Eve booted up the laptop, Caine searched through the dresser drawers. He found nothing but neatly folded clothing. No secret letters or diary.

Turning, he eyed the bed. He pulled off the covers, and checked under the plump, pale blue pillows. Still nothing. Leaning down, he checked under the bed. Nothing. Not even any dust bunnies.

As he grabbed the edge of the bed to push himself to his feet, he noticed the edge of something black poking out from between the top mattress and the box spring. He pushed the mattress aside. A black piece of paper—looking a lot like a promotional poster for an alternative rock band—lay flat on the box spring. Right next to a black bound book on vampires.

He picked up the paper by the edge to study it.

It was a promotional poster for a band calling themselves Crimson Strain. There were four members pictured. Male, varying colored spiky hair, facial piercings and dark leather accessories.

And all vampires.

Even in a photo, Caine could see that the four males were Other. It was in their eyes. They shimmered like tinsel on a Christmas tree. If a person didn't know what they were looking for, they definitely wouldn't be able to discern it. However, they would be drawn to the poster regardless. Their power wasn't in their voices like the chanteuse Nadja, but in their eyes.

"What do you have?" Eve asked.

Caine turned around and showed her the paper. "Poster for a band. A vampire band." He read the dates. "Looks like they played at Creston Community Hall a couple weeks ago."

"Whoa. That's illegal."

Caine took out a plastic evidence bag and slid the paper into it. "It sure is." He zipped it closed. "Looks like we have a few suspects to talk to now."

After tucking the evidence into his kit, Caine walked over to where Eve sat working at the girl's laptop. "Got anything?"

She nodded. "A couple of e-mails from someone named X, talking about the concert and how he really enjoyed meeting her, and can't wait to see her again. His e-mail address is vamploverX at hotmail dot com." She looked at him sideways, and arched her brow.

"Looks like we have another suspect."

"Or this X is one of our VBB members."

"VBB?"

"Yeah, vamp boy band." She grinned.

Laughter bubbled from Caine's mouth before he could stop it. Shaking his head, he rubbed a hand over his lips. "That's clever."

"I have my moments." Eve looked down at the computer and fiddled some more with the girl's e-mail account.

As she worked, trying to backtrack and find the address of vamploverX's computer, Caine watched her. She certainly did have her moments. This was one of them, when he saw past her forced bravado and glimpsed the woman behind the crime scene investigator. A woman he found to be very appealing.

She looked up, caught his gaze and held it. Once again, to Caine it felt like the room disappeared and they were alone in time. He could feel her heat embracing his body, taste her attraction on his lips. He licked them with the tip of his tongue and tasted sugar, sweet and savory.

Her face heated and she glanced back down to the keyboard, breaking the spell.

Sighing, Caine took a step back, and grabbed his

kit. "Let's go. We'll take the laptop with us and try to get the guy's address from the ISP."

She just nodded, shut the top on the computer, slid it under her arm and followed Caine. He grabbed her kit for her as they went to secure permission from the parents to take the victim's laptop.

Once they were through the front door and outside, Detective Salinas caught up with them. He put his hand on Eve's arm and stopped her from walking any farther with Caine. Caine paused at the end of the walkway and turned around, watching. He didn't like the way the detective was looking at Eve.

"Why are you doing this?" Aaron asked Eve.

"Doing what?"

"Working with *them*." He motioned toward Caine. "When I heard you had volunteered, I couldn't believe it."

She shrugged off his hand. "I volunteered to work *the case,* Aaron, nothing more."

"How does it feel working around them? I hear they have a wolfman on staff." He sniffed derisively and glanced over his shoulder at the uniform still standing at the front door to share his joke. "It's like working with an animal."

"Well, it's no different than working with you, now is it?"

Caine could smell the cop's anger intensify. Colored waves swirled by Salinas's right hand, indicating motion. Without another thought, Caine rushed toward the cop. To the humans it would seem like he transported there in front of them, his hand circling Salinas's wrist before he could raise it.

"What the hell?" Salinas took a step back, his eyes wide in shock. And fear, Caine was pleased to see.

"Don't even think about what you were about to do, Detective." Caine squeezed the man's wrist tighter.

Salinas tried to pull away, but Caine held him there. "Let go of me, freak!"

"I will, but only if you turn around and go do your job instead of interfering in Eve's."

Eve put her hand on Caine's shoulder. "Let him go, Caine."

After another tight squeeze on Salinas's wrist, Caine released his hold, but didn't step back. He wanted the detective to know that he wasn't backing away. It was one thing to insult him, but even to think about hurting Eve—there was only so much he would let slide, and that was not one of them. There were two things he hated most in the world: child abusers and crimes against women.

"Now, go back in there and ask the right questions. Get the phone number and address of this boyfriend, her other friends, then phone it into us at the lab," Caine demanded.

The detective rubbed his wrist. "I'm reporting this." He turned and rushed back into the Crawford residence.

Without a word, Caine walked back to the end of the sidewalk, picked up both kits and made his way back to the SUV. Eve ran to catch up with him. Once she was at his side, she grabbed his arm.

"What was that all about?"

"Your Detective Salinas seems to enjoy violence." Opening the back of the vehicle, he slid both kits in.

Eve set the laptop carefully into the back on a soft cushion. "The only one I saw being unnecessarily violent was you." Without looking at him, she walked along the SUV and jumped into the passenger side.

Expelling a deep sigh, Caine closed the SUV hatch. He supposed he shouldn't be surprised at her reaction. She had no idea that Detective Salinas was about to raise his hand to her. She couldn't see things the way he did. He could explain it to her, but he didn't think that she would believe him.

Caine jumped into the driver's side, and started the vehicle. He glanced at Eve. She was staring out her window, seemingly unfazed by what had transpired, but he could see her hands fidgeting in her lap.

"Why would you date a man like that anyway? He seems like a Neanderthal."

Without looking at him, she answered, "At first he was really sweet. Romantic. And he's a good cop no matter how he looks tonight." She rubbed her mouth with her hand. "I really don't want to talk about it with you, okay?"

"Okay."

He turned and watched out the front windshield as the sun started to lighten the night sky. Dawn was rapidly approaching. It wouldn't be long before it was full and glaring down. He could walk in the sunlight, but not for extended periods. Too much exposure gave him a sunburn from hell. Another reminder of how different Eve and he were. Day and night. Literally.

"How about I drop you off at your lab with the laptop. You'd be more comfortable there, tracking down his real name and address, then you can phone it in to me and we can go from there."

She swiveled in her seat and glared at him. A strong sense of hurt washed over him. He predicted her anger, but not this emotional pain.

"You can't keep me out of this case. It's mine just as much as it's yours."

"I'm not keeping you out of anything, Eve. I just thought it would be…easier if you were at your own lab."

"Easier for whom?" She sniffed.

"I thought in order to keep incidents like the one with Detective Salinas from interfering with our case it would be best to keep our involvement separate."

"I don't care what Aaron has to say." Frowning, she waved her hand around. "If I truly cared what anyone thought, I would never have volunteered. Besides, I think we're better together than we are apart." She pointed at the gearshift. "Now, put this sucker in drive and get us back to the lab. I want to catch this bastard."

"Okay."

She looked at him wryly. "Anyway, the sun's coming up. If you turn into a pile of ashes, who's going to drive the SUV?"

Smiling, Caine picked up the walkie-talkie and pressed the button to speak with the escort vehicle.

"We're heading back to Necropolis." Setting the communicator down, he put the SUV in Drive and pulled out onto the street. It was getting late and they had a killer to catch.

Chapter 11

Before Caine and Eve could step through the door to Caine's office, Baron Laal Bask was stalking down the hallway toward them, a maniacal expression on his pinched, pale face.

"Caine, we need to have a little talk." He brushed by them both and stormed into Caine's office.

The smell of fury, like the sulfur from a lit match, wafted to Caine's nose. This was obviously not going to be a pleasant conversation.

Turning to Eve, he said, "Why don't you set up in the analysis room?"

"Okay…" She hesitated, as if wanting to say more. "I'll be there when I can."

After a brief nod, she made her way down the

hall. When she was gone, Caine took a deep breath and crossed the threshold to his office.

"What's up, Laal?"

The baron whirled around on Caine, his eyes glowing like twin headlights. "Are you mad?"

Caine brushed past him, set his kit down beside his desk and sat in his high-backed leather chair. "Not that I'm aware of."

Laal leaned over the desk and pointed his long, bony finger at Caine. "You assaulted a detective. And a human one at that."

Caine returned the vampire's glare. He desperately wanted to grab Laal's finger and snap it in half. "I didn't assault him. I actually stopped him from striking Eve."

Laal let out a deep breath and backed up from the desk. "You know what, I don't care what happened. What I do care about is that their captain called Mistress Ankara and she in turn called me, yelling and screaming."

"The usual," Caine retorted as he turned on his laptop.

"She wants me to fire you, Caine."

Leaning back in his chair, Caine shook his head. "She always wants to fire me, Laal, and knows she can't. So tell me something new."

"All right." Laal sat down in the opposing chair across the desk from Caine. "The human woman is to be your lead on this case."

That brought Caine forward to lean on the desk, now acutely interested in the conversation. "I have a lead. Jace."

"Instead of being on the side, we want her on scenes collecting evidence firsthand. Mistress Ankara thinks it would be best all around if Ms. Grant is a more prominent investigator in this case."

"As in, best for her political aspirations with the human community."

Laal just gave him a tight-lipped smile. The baron didn't need to confirm or deny the statement. Caine knew exactly what Ankara Jannali was all about—domination and control.

"Eve is out of her element here. She almost got snacked on at the crime scene, for Christ's sake." Caine shook his head. "She's not ready to be the lead on this case, or any other for that matter. I've seen her personnel file. She only has two years' experience, and that is in the lab. She's still green in the field."

"Nevertheless, she is to be—"

"Jace is lead on this case," Caine interrupted. "He's earned it, and I won't take it from him to satisfy our illustrious Mistress's hard-on for politics."

Laal smiled as if he was pleased that Caine refused the suggestion. "Then I'm taking the case from you and giving it to Montgomery to head up."

"What? You can't be serious." Caine balled his hands on his desk into fists. "Monty is an incompetent ass."

"Oh, don't be melodramatic, Caine." Laal leaned back in his chair and crossed his legs, in apparent joy at rattling Caine's cage. "He's done some good work. And he's always cooperative, unlike you."

"I cooperate when the suggestion has merit. This one does not. It's a bunch of bullshit to rein me in."

"It is what it is." Laal tilted his head and smirked. "Now, do I transfer the case over to Monty?"

The baron knew all too well Caine's weaknesses. The lab was his baby. He'd spent months setting it up, getting it organized, buying the equipment. All funded by his own sizeable fortune. A vampire didn't live as long as he had and not amass some wealth. And when a man was as intelligent and inventive as Caine, that man became so rich he had more than he could logically spend. Caine had sunk nearly all of that extra money into the lab. Whether the law dictated it or not, Caine felt like he'd created the lab out of nothing, like giving birth.

Sighing, Caine slumped back into his chair. "Fine. But if she dies out there, I will tell Captain Morales that you sent her out there ill-prepared and defenseless. And your political aspirations will be destroyed."

Rising to his feet, Laal smiled. "Well, I guess it'll be your job to keep her safe then, won't it?" He brushed at his suit jacket as if flicking off dirt. "Pleasure to see you again, Caine. We miss you at the Club. You should really consider rejoining, you're looking a little tense, on edge. Nothing like a little vigorous sport to cure that." After tipping his head, Laal headed for the office door.

"Screw you," Caine grumbled right as the baron passed over the threshold.

He knew Laal had heard him by the way the vampire's shoulders flinched. But he kept on going as if Caine had said nothing.

Rubbing a hand over his face, Caine leaned on his

desk, suddenly exhausted. Sure, he'd been running purely on fumes for the past six hours. He hadn't had a decent sleep, or any sleep in the past thirty-six hours due to this case. But what exhausted him was figuring out how to explain to Jace that he was moving Eve, a human, ahead of him on the case.

He could explain the politics to the lycan, but he knew that Jace couldn't care less. All Caine's fiercest team member wanted was to follow the clues. By nature, Jace was a tracker, born and bred to follow his nose. Now Caine was going to put a barrier in front of him.

It wasn't going to be pleasant. Jace wasn't the most even-tempered person Caine knew. He could be volatile in certain circumstances, and those circumstances had now appeared.

He picked up the phone and punched in Jace's beeper number. No time like the present to engage in deadly combat with a one-hundred-and-ninety-pound lycan.

Within minutes, Jace appeared at the open door. "Hey, Chief, what's up?"

"Shut the door and take a seat."

Jace lifted a brow while he swung the door closed. "Uh-oh, what did I do now?" He stalked over to the chair and flopped down into it.

Caine leaned on his desk and looked at his investigator, unsure how to proceed. Jace had a level of unpredictability that Caine didn't like. It was probably the only reason Caine hadn't promoted him to a level three investigator. This was going to be the case that Caine would've evaluated to give him that promotion.

Jace smirked. "That bad, eh?"

"I have to place Eve on lead."

Springing forward in his seat, Jace growled, "Excuse me? I don't think I heard you right."

"I'm sorry. The baron gave me no choice in the matter."

Jace exploded out of his chair and prowled the room. "I can't believe this. An NOP comes into our lab and takes our case. What else does she want, our souls?"

Anger swelled over Caine. He didn't like the way Jace spoke about Eve. He understood the lycan's animosity toward humans. Out of them all, Jace had suffered the most, despite his claims otherwise. However, his seething hatred toward Eve made Caine want to jump out of his seat and defend her. It was irrational, but the feeling was present nonetheless.

"Jace, I understand your resentment. I feel it, too, but I would ask that you refrain from using that word in referring to Eve. She has done you no wrong, and is only here to help."

Stopping in his tracks, Jace glowered down at Caine. *"Eve is only here to help,"* he echoed. "What is the matter with you, Valorian? Are you attracted to her or something? You want to nail her, is that it?"

Before Jace even had time to blink, Caine was out of his chair and looming down at him. The urge to wrap his hand around Jace's neck surged through him violently, like a rabid fever. He had to clench his hands into fists to stop from reaching for Jace.

"This is exactly why I won't promote you, Jace. You are irrational and hotheaded. That may help you gain status in your pack, but the only thing it does here, in my lab, is create unnecessary tension and conflict."

Caine could taste the lycan's fury. It was thick and cloying, almost overpowering. But he didn't back down. He couldn't, not when confrontation was the only thing the stubborn lycan understood. In this lab, Caine was the alpha male.

Finally, after several tense minutes, Jace took a step back and dropped his gaze, indicating Caine's superiority. "I won't work under her."

"Understood." Caine nodded. "And I didn't expect you to, either. This is my lab, and I run the show. She's just going to be the star attraction for a while, like a circus act, okay?"

After a few moments, Jace's anger abated and he slowly unclenched the fists at his sides. He nodded, indicating his agreement.

Sighing with relief, Caine stepped back and sat on the edge of his desk. "Why don't you take a few hours? Go home, get some rest, eat and come back refreshed."

"Is that an order?" Jace asked, his usual humor alight in his eyes.

"Make it a strong suggestion."

"All right, Chief." He turned and reached for the door. Turning the knob, he threw it open and took a step out. Eve stood framed in the doorway, her eyes as wide as dollar coins, and a look of utter surprise on her face at running into nearly two-hundred pounds of solid lycan.

She put a hand to her chest, and took in a ragged breath. "Oh my God, you scared me."

Without a word, Jace sidestepped around her and stalked out into the hallway.

Eve watched him leave, her hands still visibly shaking. "Why does he hate me so much?"

Caine pushed away from the desk and approached her. "It's not *you* he hates. It's humanity in general he has a problem with."

"Oh well, as long as it isn't just me."

Caine smiled. The woman was a lot tougher than he gave her credit for. "What's up? You look like you have news."

Instantly her demeanor changed. Excitement filled her eyes replacing the trepidation that was there only seconds before. "I got an address off that e-mail."

"Good."

"108 Fallen Road." She glanced down at her notebook. "I did a search on the address, and it looks like a business called the Red Express."

Caine nodded. "It's a blood bar and Internet café, and not far from the Black Heart Hotel."

"A blood bar?"

"It's a place vampires can go for a…drink."

Eve's face visibly paled and he could see her neck working overtime, likely swallowing the bile rising in her throat. Her ignorance of these things frustrated him. He assumed she would've done her homework before volunteering for an assignment in his lab.

"It should be no surprise to you that vampires drink blood, Eve. It would be the same thing as ingesting milk to humans. It provides the vitamins and minerals we need to stay strong and healthy."

"I guess I never thought of it that way." She blinked up at him, an unadulterated innocence glowing on her beautiful face. A mere century ago, he would have ripped that innocence from her with his seduction. Thankfully, he had learned to control those desires, those hungers to take and devour in any way possible. But sometimes when she stood so close, intoxicating him with her delectable scent, he vehemently cursed his civility.

Turning on his heel, he marched to his desk and sat down behind it. "Well, you need to start thinking of it. This is not San Antonio, where your human sensibilities rule. This is Necropolis, where vampires drink blood, lycans fight for dominance in packs, and witches can conjure spells with a few well-placed symbols and an incantation. Violence and bloodshed are ways of life here."

She closed her notebook and looked at him as if she'd been blindsided. He supposed she had been. "You're right. I'm being naive about the situation. There is a lot I don't know or understand." She took a few steps farther into his office. "But I want to learn, and I really want to catch this guy."

Caine ran a hand through his hair as he eyed her. She was regarding him with sincerity and an eagerness he recognized in his own team members when the hunt was on for a killer. He wasn't angry with her. He was frustrated with his own reactions to her. At first, there had been distaste and annoyance at having been forced to work with her.

But now he didn't feel that way.

His anger had turned into something far more threatening to a man in his position, and far more dangerous to Eve. His growing attraction to her could only lead to disaster. And if he wasn't careful, something even worse for them both.

"Okay." He leaned back in his seat. "Blood bars don't open until sunset, so we have some time yet. Why don't you get some rest and eat something."

When she opened her mouth to protest, he put his hand up to stop her words. "There's nothing else you can do right now. Trace is working the evidence they have. Lyra's still decoding those symbols. It's not going to go any faster by hovering over them. I know. I've tried it. It doesn't work."

She smirked. "True. I've been on the receiving end of that."

"There's a cot in a separate room off the staff area if you don't want to go to your hotel. You can get some sleep."

She nodded. "I don't know if I can sleep, but maybe I could have some reading materials to pass the time?"

He stood up, swiveled around to his bookcase, and proceeded to slide out three thick volumes of Otherworld lore. He walked around the desk and set them on her outstretched arms. "Here's a little light reading for you, then."

She smiled at him over the top of the books. "Thank you."

"Don't mention it." Caine returned her smile. "If anything happens I'll find you. If not, I'll see you in a few hours."

She turned and headed for the door.

"Oh, and, Eve, stay out of Jace's way. He's a little…sensitive right now."

Glancing over her shoulder, she said, "Yeah, I kind of figured that out for myself."

He watched her leave, and then let out the breath he was holding. He hoped it wasn't a huge mistake having her on the case. The baron was risking more than he knew by demanding it. Eve was out of her element and it could prove to be hazardous not only to the case but to her own well-being.

Some Others preyed on the weaker races. And humans were at the bottom of the food chain. If it weren't for the fact that humans outnumbered the Otherworld community one thousand to one, some of the Others would take advantage of the human vulnerability.

At one time, long ago, he held that sentiment in a tight bloody fist. Vampire politics were difficult to unlearn.

Grabbing the phone off his desk, Caine dialed Mahina's number. She would need to meet them at the Red Express to hunt down their suspects and get to the truth.

A truth, Caine was starting to suspect, that no one, Otherworlder or human, was going to expect or like.

Chapter 12

Eve gulped down half her coffee as Caine maneuvered the SUV around the downtown Necropolis streets. The sultry night had settled in, and the gaudy neon signs of all-night diners and various nightclubs flashed at her as they sped by. There seemed to be no end to the oppressive heat.

Struggling with fatigue, she rubbed at her stinging eyes. She had managed to get in a few hours of sleep despite her earlier claims of not being able to. After two hours of poring through the three thick volumes that Caine had given her, exhaustion had overcome her and she had gladly succumbed to it.

She had processed a lot of information, and even now was still contemplating what she had read. She had learned more than anyone hoped to imagine about the Otherworld community and the races that made it up. *We had it all wrong.*

Eve chastised the humans that gathered the information on the various races. They had obviously taken their cue from bad horror films and cleverly written genre fiction. Nowhere had anyone mentioned the hierarchy and streamlined political system of the vampire. Nothing she had read in the primer dossiers had truly prepared her for the reality of it or of Necropolis.

"We're just about there."

Caine's voice broke into Eve's thoughts and she glanced out the window as they turned the corner onto Fallen Road. The Red Express was in a particularly seedy part of downtown. She thought Fallen Road was aptly named, given all the dilapidated buildings lined up on either side. Some of them looked like they would collapse if a sudden gust of wind blew by.

Caine pulled up in front of an unassuming brick building with a black door. There was a small sign right above the door, painted in dark red, The Red Express. After turning off the engine, he swiveled in his seat toward her, a stern expression on his face.

"You need to be really careful in here. I won't let what happened in the hotel occur here, but you need to be on your guard. Even in a place like this, vampire politics are at play."

"I know. Don't make eye contact with anyone, stay by your side, and let Captain Garner or you ask the questions. I got it." Sighing, she opened the passenger door and jumped out. What did he think she was, stupid? She remembered all too well when the vampire clerk jumped on her, his grotesque fangs drooling over her neck. The thought still gave her shivers.

She rounded the vehicle, grabbed her kit from the back and followed Caine closely as he went into the building.

The first thing that hit her when she stepped into the dimly lit bar was the metallic smell. Blood. It was overpowering—like bleach in the wash. The odor almost made her eyes water.

She sidled up next to Caine. "How can you stand it?"

He looked around, put his nose in the air and breathed. "To me it smells no different than if we were to walk into a human bar and the strong odor of beer wafted up my nose." With that, he continued into the room. Mahina was at the bar waiting for them.

As they walked, the sparse clientele watched every step. Well, Eve thought they were tracking *her* every move. She could almost feel their gazes moving over her, like fingers playing up and down a piano keyboard. Some were strictly sexual feelings, but others she could feel were far hungrier.

Subconsciously, she pressed closer to Caine, so close she could feel the solid warmth of his body.

He stopped walking, looked down at her and whispered, "I said stay close, but don't glue yourself to me."

She took a distancing step away. "I'm sorry. It's just everyone's looking at me like they want to eat me."

Caine glanced around at the patrons, then back at her and nodded. "They *do* want to eat you. Your blood probably smells like an aphrodisiac to most of them."

Her body quaked as she pictured his words in her mind. She glanced up at him. His eyes glowed just a little like white coal in a barbecue. "Do I smell like that to you?"

She didn't know why she asked, particularly at that moment, but she wanted to know. Especially with the way he was looking at her. Like she was dessert. She didn't find the thought unappealing. In fact, she liked that he looked at her like that, and that frightened her a little.

He dropped his gaze, putting it on the floor. "No." He cleared his throat. "Mahina is waiting for us, let's get this done." He continued walking. Eve followed.

Caine was lying. He couldn't look her in the eye when he answered. He was hiding his emotions from her. She wondered what his feelings encompassed. Did he just see her as food, a fresh blood supply? Or something a hell of a lot more? Either way, Eve wasn't sure if she was strong or daring enough to find out.

Mahina smiled when they approached. She shook Caine's hand, and then nodded politely to Eve.

"I showed Clive—" she pointed at the bartender "—a picture of the deceased and he doesn't recognize her. And I know he's telling me the truth because I already threatened to revoke his blood-serving license."

Clive nodded his head. "I'd remember a girl like that."

Eve noticed his fangs were extra long and that they hung over his bottom lip.

Caine slid another enlarged picture across the bar counter toward Clive. It was the one of the vampire boy band he had discovered under the victim's mattress. "Do you know any of these guys?"

Clive glanced briefly down at the photo. "Shit, yeah. That's Crimson Strain. They're in here all the time." He smiled at Caine. "They even played here once."

"Do these boys have names, by chance?"

"Sure, that's Gnash—" he pointed to each member "—J.C., Phoenix, and that's Xavier."

Eve perked up with the last name. Xavier. With a big old X. Caine glanced back at her and raised a brow. He was thinking the same thing she was. They had an Internet moniker of vamploverX. X as in Xavier? Maybe.

"Any of these guys in here right now?" Caine asked as he slid the paper back into his pocket. "If they are, please don't point, just nod in their general direction."

Clive surveyed the growing crowd. Finally, his gaze rested in the corner. The darkest corner, Eve noticed. It figures.

"In the corner. Gnash and Xavier."

"Thank you." Caine glanced at Mahina. "Let's go in nice and slow. Don't want to spook them." He glanced over his shoulder at Eve. "Stay behind me."

He didn't need to tell her. She had already slid in

behind him, with her hand on her ALS flashlight. It wasn't a gun, but somehow it made her feel better to know it was there. It hadn't stopped the skinny vampire from the hotel, but she didn't plan on letting anyone else get the jump on her like that again.

As she looked past Caine to the corner where the two men sat in the shadows, Eve wondered if they were going to run.

Seconds later, she had her answer.

Faster than she could discern, the two men were up and dashing for the back exit, clearly marked by the flashing red sign. They knocked over tables and chairs on their way across the room.

Mahina and Caine were right behind them. On instinct, Eve followed them. It was either that, or stay in the blood bar with several hungry vampires.

She pushed through the metal door and saw Mahina running down the alley one way, and Caine running the other. He glanced over his shoulder at her just as she came rushing out.

"Stay there, Eve! Don't move from that spot!" He turned and ran, disappearing around the corner onto the main street.

The moment he was gone, Eve became very aware of the shadows creeping across the alley's cracked cement walls and road. Turning around, she reached for the door handle, but found nothing but smooth painted metal. She was locked out. There was no going back in unless she walked around front and went in through the main door again.

Caine had told her to stay put, but she had foolishly left her kit on the floor near the bar. What if someone took it? There would be hell to pay if she lost all her equipment. They would need the evidence-gathering tools if they caught the suspects.

Glancing back and forth down the alley again, she made up her mind. She would quickly race around front, go in to retrieve her kit and wait for Caine by the SUV. No harm, no foul.

Sucking in a deep breath, Eve edged along the wall toward the mouth of the alley, keeping her back pressed against the gray cement. Her blouse clung to her like wet sand. The heat from the night and from a hearty dose of dread had rivulets of sweat running down her back and chest.

A clanging echoed down the road. Stopping, she glanced over her shoulder, her breath heaving in her chest. An empty pop bottle rolled across the cement.

Just a cat, Eve thought.

She swung back around and continued to creep along the wall. She got maybe another two feet, before the hair on the back of her neck rose to attention, like quills on a porcupine. Something was definitely behind her. Grasping the flashlight in her hand, she flicked it on and swiveled around pointing the light like a ray gun.

Nothing.

The space behind her was empty, except for the swirling discarded newspapers on the ground. Closing her eyes, she took a deep breath to calm her erratic breathing and her pounding heart. Her hands shook as she flicked the button off on the flashlight.

Shaking her head at her own fear, Eve turned back around to continue her way out of the alley. Maybe she was being stupid by moving. She had been relatively safe standing with her back to the door, hadn't she? And Caine did tell her to stay put. For once, she decided to do what she was told.

Her back flattened against the wall, she turned back toward the way she came. She ended up face-to-face with glowing white eyes and snarling fangs.

"Hello, gorgeous."

The flashlight was knocked out of her hand, and Eve was twisted around with a power lock around her neck. She was pulled up tight against a tall, very powerful male body. Tears of pain sprung to her eyes as he tightened his grip around her throat and shoulders.

"What's a tasty bit like you doing here?" he growled into her ear, and then laved his tongue over her lobe.

Eve struggled against him, twisting and clawing at his forearm. Even as she raked her nails across his skin, she knew it wasn't going to do any good. The man was a vampire, with inhuman strength and resistance to pain. She could tell by the way he ground his pelvis into her back that he was likely enjoying what she was doing to him. Pain was this sicko's aphrodisiac.

"Keep it up, babe. You're getting me as hard as a rock." He laughed, the sound mocking as it echoed off the walls.

"I would let her go if I were you."

Eve nearly sobbed with relief when Caine suddenly appeared in front of them. His eyes were glowing. Eve realized that they did that when he was experiencing intense emotion. Right now, he looked furious. He looked like he could rip the guy's head off with one yank.

The vampire must have sensed that Caine was no idle threat, because he did loosen his grip around her neck.

"Why should I listen to you, cop?"

"I'm not a cop, Xavier. I'm a criminalist. I'm trying to solve a horrific crime and I thought you could help me with that."

"I didn't kill anyone."

"I didn't say you did." Caine stepped to the right a little. "That woman you're holding isn't a cop, either. She's a criminalist, and my partner."

Eve stilled a little as Caine talked. He was not only calming Xavier down, but he was calming her as well. His voice was almost hypnotic. He professed not to have power in his voice, but she didn't agree. Everything about him screamed power, confidence and strength.

Xavier shivered a little. Eve could tell his resolve was softening.

"She smells human."

Caine nodded. "She is. Just like Lillian was."

Xavier stiffened. Eve thought for sure he was going to do something. She could feel the fury rising in him like mercury in a thermometer. Squeezing her eyes shut, she rammed her elbow into his stomach and shoved forward. She refused to go down without fighting.

Before she could blink, the assailant was on the ground, blood seeping from his nose, and she was trembling in Caine's arms on the other side of the alley.

Bewildered, Eve glanced over her shoulder at the fallen vampire. "I didn't do that, did I?"

Mahina appeared and rolled the vampire onto his stomach, handcuffing his hands behind his back. She had the other suspect also handcuffed and sitting on the ground.

Caine smoothed a hand down her back and shook his head. "No, but you helped. That was a great elbow."

Turning her head around, her resolve broke and the tears fell freely down her cheek. She took in a ragged breath and tried to muffle a sob.

Caine continued to stroke her back as he clutched her tighter to his body. "You're all right now, Eve. You're safe."

Unable to hold in her emotions any longer, Eve wrapped her arms around Caine, pressed her head against his chest, and cried. The fear and adrenaline flowed out of her body through her gushing tears.

All the while, Caine held her close, stroking her back, his chin nuzzled on top of her head. She fit perfectly against him, like the last link in a chain, or the interlocking piece to complete a puzzle.

She was very aware of the heat from his body. The smell of his expensive cologne tickled her nose pleasantly. And underneath that, she could detect the clean scent of his skin, soap with a hint of musk. His odor and warmth signified safety to Eve. She knew in his arms that nothing could touch her, nothing could harm her.

Even when the last of her tears fell, Eve didn't want to move. She liked being held. Enjoyed the feel of the soft cotton of his dress shirt against her cheek. It had been too long since she felt secure in another's embrace. Too long without the comfort of human contact. Although the man she sought that solace from was anything but human.

That thought forced her to move. Raising her head, she looked up at his face. His eyes no longer glowed, but there was a low burn around the iris reminding her of a lunar eclipse. His face was stern and his breath came in short pants, but she could see that it was not because he was angry.

"Are you all right?" he asked, his voice low and thick with what she hoped was desire.

She nodded, having difficulty forming any coherent words. She watched his mouth move as he spoke, suddenly and desperately wanting to press her lips to his. To feel the full softness against hers, to taste him.

She knew he could sense her desire. She could all but smell it herself, even without extraordinary abilities.

Caine raised his hand and gently stroked his fingers across her cheek. She nestled against his touch, wanting more but afraid to voice her need. Capturing a stray strand of her hair, he rubbed it between his fingers then tucked it behind her ear, like she had done on so many occasions.

"I've wanted to do that since I first met you."

She opened her mouth to protest, or to say something stupid, she wasn't sure which, but didn't have time to decide. Caine leaned down and captured her lips with his.

His lips were as soft as she'd thought they might be, though anything but gentle. He ravaged her mouth, taking, tasting and seeming to savor her with every sweep of his tongue. She couldn't catch her breath, as he demanded more from her, dipping his tongue in her mouth and nipping at her lips with his canines.

The flutters in her stomach turned into a tempest. Her knees weakened and she could barely stand as surges of pleasure rushed through her and gathered in a hot pool of desire at her center.

Finally, he broke the kiss, releasing her bottom lip from between his teeth and leaned his forehead against hers. His breath came hard and fast, mingling with hers.

"That was no simple kiss," she exhaled.

"No, it wasn't."

They stood like that, forehead to forehead, their hearts in synch, until a deep voice sounded from the mouth of the alley.

"Paramedics. Someone need help down there?"

After a deep sigh, Caine lifted his head and dropped his arms, releasing her. "We're okay, Mel. Thanks."

"Are you sure? I heard there was a tussle."

"We're good. The guy in the back of Captain Garner's car got the worst of it."

"I must've missed him." There was a pause and then, "Okay, Caine. Have a good night."

Once the paramedic was gone, Caine looked down

at her again and opened his mouth to speak. She could already see the regret on his face.

She put her hand up. "Don't you dare apologize. I'll hate myself if you do."

"I wasn't going to apologize, Eve. I was going to say that I'm afraid that this was reckless and inappropriate on my part."

Eve took a distancing step back and rubbed a hand over her face. "You know that was a hell of a lot worse than an apology." Shaking her head, she smoothed a hand over her shirt then lifted her chin. "I'm going to go get my kit from inside. I'll meet you at the car."

She didn't wait for his response. At the moment, with anger now whirling around with desire, she was in no mood to hear anything he had to say. He had taken a perfect, beautiful kiss and sullied it with an uptight explanation for his actions.

She knew he desired her; there had been no mistaking that fact. Would it kill the undead bastard just to say so?

Chapter 13

He watched them from his perch on top of the roof of the neighboring building. They had no idea that he was there. He could move virtually undetected, but he could see and hear them as plain as day.

When the human woman came out of the alley and around the front of the bar, he tracked her with his eyes. She was attractive in a purely human way, he supposed. Full breasts and hips, long shapely legs, round expressive eyes in a comely face. Not his usual taste in a sexual partner. He liked them skinny, fragile, breakable. But cowed the right way, she might be an enticement. She had more guts and strength then he first gave her credit for.

Although sex was not his main reason for wanting

her, he found himself growing heavy with desire, with hunger. No, she would be perfect for other, more culinary, reasons. He could almost taste her blood on the tip of his tongue.

When she disappeared into the Red Express, he turned his attention to Caine Valorian as he came out of the alley and walked toward the SUV parked on the street. The werewolf captain's sedan was long gone, and his initial quarry had already come and gone.

The vampire was proving to be more of a problem than expected. He had underestimated Caine's abilities, both as an investigator and as a predator. The vampire hid himself well under all that polish and self-righteous indignation. He suspected that if pushed, Caine would reveal his true colors. Those of a bloodthirsty killer.

Smiling, he wondered how far he could push the vampire. Maybe if he used the right bait, he could turn Caine into an ally instead of an enemy.

Killing him would be far more satisfying that way.

Chapter 14

Caine popped a breath mint into his mouth while he watched from behind the two-way mirror as Detective Mahina interrogated Xavier. The other one, Gnash, lawyered up immediately, so they had got nothing from him.

So far, the only thing Xavier owned up to was playing a gig across city lines after curfew. A misdemeanor offense, but at least it was enough to hold him for a few hours while the lab processed his DNA to see if it matched what they'd recovered from the victim. They also checked the prints they pulled from the band poster in her room.

From the way Xavier had reacted when Caine had said the victim's name, he figured the suspect knew her. It was just a matter of how well. They weren't able to get any clean prints from the hotel room, so his DNA, if a match, was the only thing they had to link him to the victim's death. He might have known her, but Caine wasn't sure if he had killed her.

Caine glanced to his right, risking a look at Eve as she watched the interrogation. She hadn't said two words to him since they'd arrived back at the lab. He couldn't blame her. He had acted like a complete idiot in the alley.

When he'd seen her in the suspect's grip, tears staining her cheeks, he'd nearly lost his self-control. Rage, pure and intense, surged through him like a brush fire. He had wanted to tear the boy's throat out. And when he finally was able to rescue her and had her safe in his arms, he found he didn't want to let go. She had felt so right in his arms, pressed against his body.

He hadn't been able to resist kissing her, tasting her on his lips.

And when he finally did, it was like an explosion rushed through him. One feeling was indistinguishable from another. He had wanted to take her, right there. Pick her up and ram her back into the cement wall, so he could ravage her, plunging himself into her until they both screamed.

Even now the urge to touch her itched at his palms. What was it about her that made him respond this way? So primal and unthinking. He'd spent the last few decades conditioning himself against these urges, but here they were, threatening to escape no matter how hard he tried to rein them in.

Clenching his hands into tight fists, he returned his attention to the interrogation room, where it was safe.

"We found this in Lillian Crawford's room." Mahina slid the promo poster wrapped in an evidence bag across the table toward Xavier. He barely glanced at it.

"So?"

"It has your prints on it."

He smirked. "Yeah, I handed them out before the concert. Doesn't prove shit. I must've handed out over two hundred of them."

Mahina leaned across the table. "I have confirmation that Lillian was at your concert and she did talk to you."

Xavier glanced down, and Caine could see his right leg bobbing up and down as if on a spring.

"I talked to lots of chicks." He smirked. "Why do you think I'm in a band?"

"Well, I don't care about the other chicks. I care about just one." She slid the photo of Lillian across the table again. She tapped the photo. "This one." Keeping her finger on the photo, she asked, "Do you want to amend your statement that you don't know her?"

"I might have talked to her. So what?"

"So what is she's dead."

Xavier looked at the photo and started to chew his bottom lip. "I didn't kill her."

"But you knew her, right?"

"Yeah, maybe."

Mahina slammed her hand on the table. Xavier jumped. Caine even flinched.

"Yeah or maybe? Which is it?"

"Yeah, I knew her, okay. I talked to her for a while at the concert and that's it."

"Did you have sex with her?"

"No," he answered.

"Are you sure you didn't bite her?"

"I'm sure."

"So your DNA isn't going to match the DNA we pulled from her neck, right? You're not lying to me, are you, Xavier?"

He shook his head.

Mahina leaned back in her chair. "Are you vamploverX?"

Lifting his head, he stared at her. "What?"

"VamploverX, isn't that your screen name?"

"No."

"He's lying," Eve blurted out.

Caine glanced at her. She hadn't taken her eyes off the suspect. "Maybe. But we need to prove it." He turned back to the room.

Mahina smiled. "Ah, come on, you're going to tell me you don't go by vamploverX? I mean look at you, you're a good-looking guy, in a band, and your name starts with *X*." She pushed to her feet and started to pace around him.

Caine knew she was just getting her groove on. He'd seen Mahina do her moves so many times before, it was as if he could predict her actions before she thought of them.

"Let me tell you what I think, Xavier. I think you met Lillian at the concert. I think you liked her, or at least knew you could manipulate her since she was just a silly little human girl and she thought you were so dark and sexy." She paused for effect, and then continued. "I think she gave it up to you that night and you knew an easy mark, so you started e-mailing her, knowing she was hooked on your darkly mysterious ways. You told her to meet you somewhere close to the edge of town, you picked her up, smuggled her into the city, took her to a hotel, screwed her and then sucked the life from her."

"No!" Xavier shot forward, his hands grasping the tabletop. "That's not how it happened."

Mahina rounded him and sat on the edge of table near him. "Then tell me how it did happen."

"I want a lawyer."

Sighing, Mahina slid off the table. "Okay. I'll just pop out, get you that lawyer and check with the lab to see if your DNA match is in yet." She walked to the door, and then glanced over her shoulder at him. "Don't go anywhere." She knocked once, and the door opened.

Caine continued to keep an eye on Xavier as Mahina left the room and made her way to the little room where Caine and Eve were watching.

The door opened, and Mahina slid in. "What do you think?"

"I don't know. He's lying about something."

"I agree, but I don't think he killed her."

Caine nodded. He didn't think so, either. The

vampire was certainly capable of it, as they all were, but he seemed affected by the scenario Mahina had spelled out for him. Guilt maybe? Remorse? But over what? That she was dead or that he'd been caught?

"He may not have killed her, but he's involved somehow." Eve turned and glanced at Caine.

He agreed. Nodding, he was about to say something, when the beeper in his pocket vibrated. He took it out and glanced at the message. "The lab. The results must be in."

"Well, let's go get them." Mahina motioned toward the room. "He's not going anywhere anytime soon."

Minutes later, Caine, Eve and Mahina gathered in Gwen's lab eagerly waiting for the results.

Gwen handed the paper to Caine. He didn't need to read it to know what it said. They had the wrong person. "No match to the DNA or the hair."

Mahina shook her head. "Damn. I was hoping we had him."

"Yeah, I think we all did." Caine sighed. "It would be nice to have this case wrapped up neat and tidy, but my gut tells me we aren't going to get that lucky."

"He may not have had sex with her that night or bitten her, but he was involved." Eve pushed away from the table she was leaning against. "Maybe he was the lure."

Caine looked at her, eyebrow raised. "What makes you say that?"

"The e-mails on her computer. I checked the ones in her send file, the ones she sent to him. Very eager,

very…smitten, I guess is the word. She was definitely attracted to him. She wanted to be with him."

He nodded, now eager they were on the right
track. "Yes. Yes, that's good. Were there any notes
about meeting him somewhere? Maybe if we can
find the place she was picked up at, we can trace her
path to the city."

"Not that I could see. She might have been instructed to delete the note after she received it."

"Can we trace the message from his account?"

"If I could get into the account…"

Caine slid his phone out of his pants pocket. "I'll
get us a warrant and access." He glanced at Gwen.
"Thanks for the quick work."

She grunted and went back to work.

He looked at Mahina, then at Eve. "Okay, we're at
least moving. I'll get Jace to get on our trace evidence
and see where our fibers and wire lead us, and see if
our witch has deciphered those symbols yet." Caine
turned to leave the lab, Mahina leading the way.

"Wait," Eve called after him. He stopped and
looked at her. "We're not letting him go, are we?"

Caine could see the unasked question on her face.
She was still shaken up from the incident in the alley.
He could tell by the welling concern in her eyes that
she thought they would let the vampire go even after
he had assaulted her. There was no way in hell Caine
was going to let that slide. Xavier had hurt Eve, and
he would pay for it one way or another.

"No. I'm asking for charges. No one assaults a
crime scene investigator and walks away from it."

She nodded at him. "Thank you." Pulling her gaze away, she glanced down at the floor. "I'll go pore over her laptop again. Maybe there's something I missed. I'll also see what Detective Salinas found out from her friends and the boyfriend." Without looking at him, she brushed by him and out the door. As she passed, she gently squeezed his arm then just as quickly let go and continued down the hallway.

He watched her go.

Mahina cleared her throat. "Um, is there something you want to talk about?"

Swiveling his gaze to her, he frowned. "What do you mean?"

Mahina motioned toward Eve, who had just disappeared into the analysis room. "Blondie. You're not the only one that can sense feelings, you know."

"Can we go do our jobs, Garner?"

She put her hand on his arm to stop him from walking away. "You're attracted to her."

Caine shrugged off her touch and frowned. "I am not."

"The fact that you can't look at me tells me you are, and you know it."

Lifting his gaze, he glared at the lycan detective. "I'm looking at you, Mahina. Can we get on with our jobs now and solve this blasted case?"

"Be careful, is all I'm saying." She patted him on the shoulder. "As a friend."

He smirked. "Mahina, you don't have friends, remember?"

"Oh, yeah." She grinned. "Sorry I said anything."

She slapped him hard on the back, and then walked away humming the theme to *Jaws*.

He wanted to tell her to go to hell, tell her that she didn't know what she was talking about. But she was right. He needed to tread lightly. He was nearing dangerous territory with his emotions. Soon, they would start clouding his judgment. And he refused to let that happen.

Without his keen senses and intuition, he wouldn't be doing this lab any good. And Eve was starting to interfere with that. He was starting to care about her in a way that made the case come second.

He couldn't let that happen. He wouldn't. Not after all he'd worked for, all he had done for this lab. The sooner they solved this case, the sooner Eve would be gone. And he could carry on with his life—uncomplicated and with a singular purpose—to collect evidence and solve crimes.

Chapter 15

Head down, Eve marched down the corridor toward the analysis room. As she walked, she had the distinct sensation of being watched. When she neared the open door, she looked up and spied Kellen down the hall leaning against another doorjamb, eyeing her.

She met his gaze, expecting him to smile, but he just watched her with a slight twitch in his upper lip. She had the distinct feeling of being ogled from head to toe. His gaze was not of friendly interest but one of predatory lust.

She quickly dropped her gaze and stepped into the room. She pulled up short when she saw Lyra at the computer, looking at magical symbols projected in large format on the wall.

"I'm sorry. I didn't realize anyone was in here."

"No worries."

"I need to go over the laptop again. Is it going to bother you if I work in here, too?"

"Knock yourself out," Lyra said without looking at Eve, as she flipped to another symbol.

Eve settled herself at the smaller table behind Lyra's workstation. Trying to shake the creepy sensations left by Kellen's gaze, she opened up the laptop and attempted to access Lillian's e-mail account. Maybe she could recover all the e-mails sent to her address even though Lillian had deleted them from her in-box. They still could be in the system somewhere.

After a half hour of trial and error, Eve couldn't find any e-mails in the victim's computer that had been requests for a meeting. All she could find were several notes from vamploverX claiming how much he liked Lillian and had enjoyed talking with her at the concert. Although Xavier hadn't confessed to being vamploverX, there was no doubt in Eve's mind that he was. She'd have to wait until they had a warrant before she could access that particular Hotmail account.

Now she had to call Detective Salinas, which she dreaded more than working a grisly crime scene. She could just imagine what her former lover was going to say about Caine and the situation that had transpired at the Crawfords'.

Sliding her cell phone out from her purse, she dialed his number and waited with a lump forming in her throat.

He picked up after three rings. "Salinas."

"Aaron, it's Eve."

The silence on the other end was like an icy fog. She shivered involuntarily just picturing Aaron's stern expression on the other end.

"I wanted to know if you talked with Lillian Crawford's boyfriend and her friends."

"Yeah, I did."

"And?" It was like pulling teeth with him. He had always been a stubborn son of a bitch. Macho to a fault.

He hadn't started out like that. She had fallen for him initially because of the respectful way he had dealt with her once on a crime scene she attended, and it hadn't hurt that he possessed those dark Latin looks coupled with a hard, muscled body. After meeting her on the scene, he had sent flowers to the lab every day for a week until she agreed to go out with him.

A month later, the flowers stopped and so had the respect.

"The boyfriend confirmed that she was starting to hang out with this Goth crowd. The last time he spoke to her was on the phone Tuesday morning. They were supposed to hook up later at the mall, but she never showed. He thought she was just playing games and it never crossed his mind to track her down or call her parents. He started to get worried by Wednesday afternoon when he hadn't heard from her. That was when he called her parents and they reported her missing."

Eve wrote as he spoke. "And the friends?"

"They confirmed the vic was at the Creston Community Hall a couple of Saturdays ago at the concert with this Crimson Strain group. One of her friends, Sarah Hamilton, says that she saw the vic speaking to at least two or three of the band members and the roadies. She pointed them out on the band poster I had. I circled the ones she identified."

"Good. Could you fax me a copy of that?"

"Sure."

"Thanks, Aaron."

"So, this Crimson Strain band, are they vamps too?"

"Yes." Eve didn't like the sound of disgust in his voice. She had a feeling the conversation was going in a direction she wasn't going to like.

"What's it feel like to be surrounded by them? Are you scared that they might eat you?"

"Aaron, I'm not going to answer that. Thank you for the information. I'll call you if anything else develops."

"Why, are you afraid I'm going to find out you're sleeping with Valorian?"

Sighing, she clenched her jaw and tried hard not to scream into the phone. "Aaron, even if I was, it would be none of your business. You lost your privileges to care whom I sleep with. Goodbye."

Flipping her phone closed, she set it on the table and rubbed at the spot on her forehead where a headache was throbbing. Thankfully, she had hung up on him before he had a chance to call her a whore. He had once before, after they broke up.

She couldn't figure out why he thought that way, but she had never understood him. That was one of the reasons their short relationship was doomed to failure. They barely talked, and when they did, Aaron was always telling her she should give up her criminalist career for something more suited to her disposition. Meaning her gender. Like waitress, or bank teller, or nurse.

She had told him to shove his advice and never to talk to her about it again. A week later, their affair ended.

Sighing, she ran a hand over her face and glanced up at Lyra to see if she had heard her conversation. The witch hadn't as much as moved from her position behind the computer. Eve mumbled a thank-you under her breath.

Eve looked up at the displayed drawings on the wall. Lyra clicked to another one. Eve eyed it curiously. There was something about it that seemed familiar to her. The looping tail. The point at the end of it. It looked like a serpent's tail.

Lyra flipped to the next slide.

"Wait. Go back," Eve blurted out, excitement coursing through her.

Lyra turned and stared at her, a questioning look on her face.

"I recognize something about that symbol."

Lyra flicked it back once.

Eve stood up and walked to the wall. "What are these symbols used for?"

"Either a spell or summoning a spirit."

She traced the line of the tail with her finger. "It's a tail. A serpent's tail." Cocking her head to the side, she scrutinized the rest of the symbols. She put her finger on the three points with circles on top. "Three heads." Then she moved her finger over to a looping that looked like a squished letter B. "And the letter B."

She took a few steps back, putting her hand on her hip. "I could be wrong but I think this is the symbol for—"

"Balam," Lyra finished for her.

Eve turned and nodded at Lyra. "Yes. From the Key of Solomon."

Lyra knocked herself in the forehead. "Damn it! Why didn't I see that?"

"Sometimes when we get too close, we can't see anything," Eve offered.

Lyra looked up at the wall again. "These markings on her body were not a spell, but a summoning. A demon summoning." Her gaze then settled on Eve. "How did you know? This isn't exactly everyday knowledge, especially for—"

Shrugging her shoulders, Eve answered, "I was bored in university and took a demonology course for fun."

"For fun?"

"Yeah, I've always been enthralled with the occult and certain mythologies, like, well, vampires, werewolves and such." She cleared her throat, feeling uncomfortable.

Lyra flipped through the rest of the markings. Eve watched them flash by on the wall one by one, a sense of dread washing over her with each picture.

"So they were really trying to call Balam forth?"

Eve asked. "Why would they do that? Demons aren't real, are they?"

The witch was staring at the wall, at one symbol in particular—a crescent-moon shape with two arrows and another shape Eve couldn't discern.

Lyra seemed pensive as she chewed on her bottom lip, but something flashed across her face that Eve had not expected. Fear.

Before Lyra could answer Eve's question, Jace popped his head into the room. "Meeting in the staff room in five minutes." He was gone again just as quick.

Eve wandered back to her workstation, shut down the laptop and started for the door. She glanced over her shoulder at Lyra, who was still flipping through slides, her face a mask of determination. "Are you coming?"

Lyra waved her hand in the air. A dismissal if Eve ever saw one. She walked out of the room and started down the hall toward the staff room. As she neared the glassed-in room, Eve noticed she didn't have her purse with her. She turned and walked back to the analysis room.

She stopped a foot from the door when she heard Lyra's voice.

"Gran, you could've offered some help on the symbols, you know."

Eve risked a peek. Leaning forward she looked around the door frame and into the room.

Lyra was still standing at the computer but now her chin was lifted a little and looked like she was eyeing something floating above her.

"I know you knew what these symbols meant. A little help once in a while would be appreciated." Lyra shook her head and waved her arms in the air. "What do you mean Eve needed a break? Whose side are you on?"

Eve decided that it wouldn't likely be a good time to barge into the room with Lyra conversing with her dead grandmother. At first, Eve had thought the little brunette was mad, but the longer she'd been here and the more she'd seen, the more she was starting to believe.

She would clear her throat to let Lyra know someone was coming so she didn't think Eve was rude walking in on her private conversation.

However, she didn't get the chance to.

Lyra turned to the door. "You might as well come in. Gran says you've been standing there long enough."

Face blushing bright pink, Eve stepped into the room. "I'm sorry, I didn't mean to intrude on your… conversation."

"Don't sweat it. Even Caine has a hard time accepting that I talk with my dead granny."

Sheepishly, Eve glanced around the room. "Can you see her, too?"

Lyra shook her head. "No. I just hear her as plain as I do you. Sometimes when she's angry, I can get a glimmer, but it usually doesn't materialize into a recognizable shape."

"I see."

Lyra sniffed. "It's okay if you don't believe it,

Eve. Not believing in something doesn't make it any less real."

A cool draft blew over Eve making shivers run down her back. Rubbing her arms and eyeing the room for a suspicious glimmer, she nodded. "I'm starting to realize that more and more every day."

Lyra smiled.

It was the first genuine smile she'd seen from the petite witch. Its warmth and generosity made her return it in kind. Somehow, she felt as if she had just made a friend.

Lyra motioned toward the door. "We shouldn't keep Caine waiting. He can get grumpy."

Eve grabbed her purse from the floor near the workstation and slung it over her shoulder. "Really? I just can't see him as grumpy."

"Oh, just wait. Give him some more time. You'll see it, and it ain't pretty."

Smiling, Eve followed Lyra out the door.

Chapter 16

How odd, Caine thought, that Eve and Lyra walked into the staff room together, seemingly relaxed. They sat on the remaining seats on the sofa, side by side. Those were the last two people—well maybe Jace was the last person—that he ever thought to see being friendly with one another.

Jace was leaning against the table, Givon had joined them and was perched in one of the wooden chairs at the long lunch table, and Mahina paced around the room like a caged animal. Kellen was MIA.

His unusual mismatched team was assembled.

Pushing off the counter he had been leaning on, Caine took control of the room. "All right, we need to lay out what we have and brainstorm where we need to go. We need to close this case. The baron is paging me every half hour, and I don't like it." He eyed everyone in the room. "Who wants to start?"

"While Lyra was reviewing the markings left on the victim's body, I happened to recognize a symbol from a demonology course I took in university. The one for a nasty demon named Balam."

Everyone turned toward Eve.

"Demonology? Interesting," Caine remarked.

Lyra took up the thread when Eve glanced at her. "I don't know why I didn't see it earlier, but the markings on the victim's chest are indicators of a demon summoning." She glanced around the room at everyone. "They used the victim as a human blood sacrifice to call Balam forth. It's one of two ceremonies needed to summon the entity to this world."

"Who's Balam?" Jace asked.

"He's one of the seventy-two demons that King Solomon evoked and imprisoned to be used for his own purposes," Eve started.

Lyra continued, "He's a terrible, great and powerful king of demons that commands forty legions. He supposedly can see the past, present and future and can make men invisible."

Caine felt a ripple of fear pass through the room. He glanced at Givon and saw his old friend fidget in his seat. Odd. He didn't think Givon was afraid of anything.

"Did the summoning work?" Jace asked.

"I don't know. They'd have to do another ceremony to complete the cycle," Lyra answered.

Jace snorted. "Well, we wouldn't want a demon running around Necropolis."

"I wouldn't joke about it, Jace. Demon summoning is serious business."

"Get real, Lyra. Demons?"

Lyra shook her head, and leaned back against the sofa. "This from a werewolf."

Caine put his hand up to stop the squabbling he could sense coming. "Okay, let's just stick to the evidence, please. We can hear theories later." He nodded to Eve. "What did Detective Salinas have to say?"

"He talked to Lillian's friends and boyfriend, and they all confirmed that she was starting to hang around with the Goth community, that they all went to the concert put on by Crimson Strain, and they all identified Xavier as one of the band members she talked to. They also said that she'd been having a weird fascination with vampires lately, and had been doing a lot of research."

"Hence, the poster and book we found under her mattress in her room," Caine added for the benefit of the room.

Nodding, Eve continued. "I went through that entire laptop, and didn't find one note asking Lillian to meet anyone. Just lots of e-mail flirting between her and vamploverX. We still haven't confirmed for sure Xavier is vamploverX."

Caine turned to Jace. "What do you have?"

"Trace came back on the fibers and the wire. Fibers are from a burgundy carpet, a vehicle carpet, number 4305 Oxblood to be exact, option for G10 Chevy vans, from 1983 to 1995."

"What do our suspects drive?" Caine asked Mahina.

She flipped open her notebook. "A red 2000 Pontiac Grand Am, and a silver Toyota Tercel. No other vehicles registered to either of them."

"And the wire?"

"Standard copper wire. Used in anything from electrical generators and motors, electrical wiring, electronic goods, home heating systems, computers, motor vehicle radiators and air conditioners."

"Also copper jewelry," Lyra pointed out.

"Was the vic wearing any copper jewelry, Givon?"

The coroner shook his head. "No, just a diamond pinkie ring and a silver ankle bracelet."

"Where does Xavier work?" Caine asked.

"Bartender at Howler, 2617 Moonglow Road," Mahina read off her notes.

"And Gnash?"

"Dishwasher at the same place."

"And they're both guitarists in Crimson Strain," Eve added. "They play *electric* guitars."

Caine nodded. "Good call, Eve."

"But neither one owns a van," Jace pointed out, obviously eager to debunk anything Eve suggested.

"Maybe we're looking at the wrong band member?" Lyra offered.

Caine glanced at Mahina. "Do we have enough to pull the others in?"

She flipped open her notebook again, swiftly turning the pages. "I'm sure I can make a good argument for it."

"Let's talk to them all to make sure we have all

our bases covered. Maybe someone is using Xavier as a front."

After shutting her notebook, Mahina nodded. "I'll track them down. I'll call when I have something for you."

"Thanks, Mahina," Caine said.

With a slight tilt of her head, the detective left the staff room to complete her task.

When she was gone, Caine paced around the room, pondering their evidence and where it led. He glanced at each member of his team as he strolled past. "Okay what do we need to know?"

"We need to find the van," Jace remarked.

"Yes." He nodded at Jace. "See if we can get access to the cameras at the checkpoints. We can at least narrow it down to when she had to have been brought in. We can go through the footage. Maybe we'll get lucky and see the van."

"On it."

"Now that I know the right symbols," Lyra glanced appreciatively at Eve, "I can track down which ceremony they were doing and why. I have some contacts that dabble in the dark arts. Maybe they've heard something."

"The drugs in her system," Givon offered. "Where did they come from?"

"Good question, Sil." Caine walked the room again. "V can be bought on any side street. It's the heparin that's the key here. There haven't been any pharmaceutical thefts or break-ins reported, so that leaves us with someone with access. This is a big list that we don't have access to. So we'll have to move on from there for now."

"I guess I'll keep at the communication between vamploverX and Lillian," Eve offered.

He nodded to her. "You'll have your access by the end of the day."

"Good."

"But before we move forward, we need to recharge our batteries. Everyone here has been working twenty-four hours. If you can do it, take a few hours and go home, shower, eat, relax and then come back with fresh eyes and brains."

Jace pushed away from the table. He nodded to Caine as he passed toward the exit. "I'll see you in a few."

Lyra stood up. "I'm going to go feed my cat, and make some calls." She smiled at Eve, then left the staff room.

When everyone had filed out of the room, Eve remained seated on the sofa. She glanced at Caine and raised a brow in question.

"I'll drive you to your hotel."

She nodded. "Okay, I could probably do with a shower."

As she brushed past him to go out the door, he scented her. He didn't think she needed a shower at all. She still smelled like plums and vanilla, an odor he was coming to crave as much as the oxygen in the air.

Chapter 17

Pink and orange streaked the eastern skyline as the SUV drove over the deserted city streets. As the buildings rolled by, Eve put a hand to her mouth to stifle a yawn. She didn't want to admit it, but she was bone-tired. She hadn't worked this long a day in her last two years of investigating. But she'd never been on such an important case before. A career-defining case.

When Caine pulled the vehicle to a halt in front of an elegant hotel, she was even too weary to be impressed. The doorman opened her door and she slid out. Before she could consider it, Caine was out of the vehicle and removing her bag from the trunk.

"Thanks." She reached for her suitcase. He held it firm.

"I'll get you settled."

She gave him a brief nod. "Okay."

She had to admit she was pleased that he was going up with her. At this point, she didn't know if she could even handle her key card.

As they stepped into the posh lobby, Caine took her arm and steered her toward the elevators. She didn't protest. She was thankful for his guidance. Another time, she would've insisted on carrying her bag and going her own way, but not this morning, not in this place.

The elevator doors opened and they stepped in. Caine pushed the button for the eighth floor. As the elevator ascended, Eve stared straight ahead, her eyes hot and sore. Lifting her hand, she rubbed at them. She was getting more tired by the minute. The drone of the elevator didn't help matters.

With a happy ring, the doors opened and Caine stepped out. She followed him down the wide hall to her room. He slid the key card down the door lock, and pushed open the door. Turning, he handed her her bag.

"There you go."

As she reached for the bag, her fingers brushed against his. Instantly her gaze lifted and met his. Heat swirled around her and she had the sudden urge to nuzzle into the crook of his arm and let him steer her into the room. Was that the vampire lure working? Or was it more? She didn't care to figure it out at this point.

"Would you…" She paused and cleared her throat.

"Would you come in and wait for me? I'd only like to shower and eat before heading back."

Without a word, he nodded and swept his arm toward the door, motioning for her to enter first. She did and she was acutely aware of his presence behind her as he followed her through. He shut the door behind them. The sound of the lock engaging clanged in her ears like an alarm, warning her of the danger ahead. But she ignored it. She was too tired to fight. After all that had happened so far, she didn't want to be alone. If she allowed herself the luxury of isolation, she just might succumb to it and break down. And she feared she wouldn't be able to get up and leave the room again.

Carrying her bag, she wandered through the large suite and found the bedroom. She set her bag on the bed, and then peered around the doorway into the sitting room. Caine was seated on the sofa, straight backed and stiff, looking as tense and unnerved as she was.

"I'll just jump in the shower."

He nodded. "Do you want me to order up some food?"

"Sure."

"What would you like?"

"Anything edible. Oh, and coffee. Strong black coffee."

"That I can do." He chuckled.

Eve wandered back to the bed, dug through her bag, grabbed her shampoo, and went into the bathroom. She quickly shed her clothes, opened the glass shower door and stepped in, closing it behind her. As she turned on the water, tingles of acute awareness prickled her skin.

She closed her eyes as the hot water sluiced over her skin, instantly releasing the achy tension that had settled into her muscles. Rotating her shoulders, she let her head fall back. Water sprayed over her face, slightly relieving the headache that brewed at her temples. Turning, she soaked her hair. Reaching for her shampoo, she squeezed some into her palm and smoothed it down the wet surface of her head. As she massaged the soap into her scalp, she thought of the way Caine had reacted to the smell of her shampoo. While the bubbles cascaded down her skin, she questioned if he would be able to discern it on her flesh. She wondered if he could smell her as she washed. Was he thinking of her naked and wet?

Grabbing the soap, Eve slid it over her shoulders and down her arms, reveling in the feel of it slick against her skin. Gradually she made her way over her torso, across her belly and up to her breasts. While she rubbed the soap over her nipples, she again thought of Caine's hands and the way they would feel on her flesh, pulling and pinching her peaks between his strong fingers. She gasped as clear images of Caine kneeling at her feet, his fingers possessing her body and his mouth claiming her breasts slammed into her.

The thoughts were so intense she snapped open her eyes and glanced down to make sure it was not real and only imagined. That he hadn't snuck into the bathroom unaware, stripped and climbed into the shower with her.

She rubbed at the glass shower door to see if he was standing in the doorway watching her. His presence had been so powerful, she swore that he was right next to her, looking at her, touching her. But as she peered through the steamed glass door, she saw that she was still alone.

Sighing with relief, Eve shut off the water, wrung out her hair and opened the shower door. As she stepped out, she reached for a towel and wrapped it around her body. She took another and wrapped her hair in it on top of her head. When she glanced in the mirror, she noticed how flushed her face was. Turning on the tap, she splashed cold water onto her face. Maybe the icy freshness would jolt her from her thoughts.

She found the more she was around Caine, the more she liked and respected him. He was a fantastic investigator, with a keen eye for detail. And he led his team with elegance and dignity. She had an affinity for men in authority. Her father had been a police officer, a decorated sergeant, before he succumbed to cancer. Her lovers were often men of rank and power. Even in the academy, she had ongoing fantasies for one of instructors. Male power was a commanding aphrodisiac for her.

She liked how Caine never needed to use his power, it was just there hovering around him like a hot swirling aura. Everyone could feel it, sense it, some could probably even see it, and therefore there was never a need for him to brandish it.

Shutting off the water, she took her hair down out of the towel and rubbed it dry. She would run a comb through it, and put it back in a ponytail. Plain and simple. Maybe if she dressed down, it wouldn't feel like Caine was devouring her from head to toe. Ever since they had shared that incredible kiss in the alley, she could sense a purely sexual vibe from him. One that he was constantly fighting.

After hanging up the towel, Eve wandered back into the bedroom, rummaged through her bag, took out a T-shirt and khaki pants and got dressed. Squaring her shoulders, she stepped out into the sitting room.

Caine tried not to stare as Eve walked out of the bedroom. He had been sitting on the sofa thumbing through a coffee-table book of landscape photography, forcing his mind away from the fact that she was in the shower, naked, wet…and vulnerable. He could taste her vulnerability on his tongue.

Before she reentered the room, he had sworn to himself that he would remember that she was tired, stressed and not an object of his increasing desire.

Then she walked into the room, looking so alluring, he had to fight to remember his earlier vow.

So instead, he turned his attention to the food that room service had wheeled in only moments ago. With flair, he removed the two metal coverings. Steam erupted from underneath. "I didn't know what you liked for breakfast, so I ordered everything on the menu."

Laughing, she neared the carts, plucked a plump, ripe strawberry from the fruit tray, and took a bite. He couldn't help but watch as the juice stained her lips crimson. He wanted to lean forward and trace the line of her sensuous mouth with his tongue.

"Oh God, this tastes heavenly," she exclaimed as she collapsed onto the sofa. "I usually survive on coffee and a bagel with cream cheese."

Enjoying her obvious pleasure, Caine wheeled the carts to the sofa so she could reach without standing. "Then this should just about kill you." Chuckling, he joined her on the sofa, snatching a ripe piece of cantaloupe for himself. "I'm a tea and eggs on toast man myself. Anything that's quick but gives me energy to last twenty-four hours or more."

Popping the rest of the fruit into her mouth, she eyed him. "You seem like a tea guy."

"Oh, so I'm pompous, uptight and cold, am I?"

Grabbing another strawberry, she said, "Hmm, more like reserved, refined and—" she paused in thought "—pensive."

"Pretty words for the same thing, I think."

Eve grabbed the plate of pancakes, poured syrup on them, and set them on her lap. "I don't think you're cold or pompous."

"Uptight?" he asked as he dug into the scrambled eggs.

After she took a bite of pancake, she nodded, a wry smile forming on her lips. "Maybe a little."

He smiled. "Well, thank you."

"You're welcome." She took another healthy bite from her plate.

For the next half hour, they ate in silence, enjoying the piles of food that Caine had ordered. He couldn't remember the last time he'd enjoyed a meal so much. He felt at ease with Eve. He didn't have to project an air of power or authority. He could let down his guard a little and relax. She seemed to feel the same. He could sense her easiness with him. That pleased him greatly.

After they were done devouring the food, they both leaned back against the sofa, contented. Eve turned to look at him. "I don't think I've ever eaten that much. Not since I was a kid."

"Me, either. Actually, I don't think I've ever eaten that much."

She smiled at him, but he could tell she was pondering over something she wanted to ask him. "You can ask me," he said.

"What?"

"Whatever it is that is causing those lines creasing your brow."

She rubbed at the spot Caine indicated. "How old are you exactly?"

"I've been a vampire for two-hundred and fifty-four years." He sighed, resting his head back on the sofa cushions, mimicking her position. "But I was born in 1711."

She stared at him for a long while. He wished he could read her mind and find out what she was thinking. For the first time in so long he could barely remember, he worried what another person thought of him.

"You look pretty good for being close to three-hundred. Hardly a wrinkle in sight."

He laughed. "Thank you. It's the coenzyme Q10 I take every day."

She joined him in the laughter. It felt good to laugh. Caine had always believed that it was a person's ability to laugh even in the direst circumstances that kept them sane.

"What's it like?" she asked after her laughter had faded. "How often do you need to—"

"Feed?"

She nodded.

"I take blood once a week. I don't drink from a person anymore. I get mine straight from a bottle. O positive packaged and shipped to a Necropolis grocery store just up the street from where I live." He put his feet up on the coffee table as he continued to talk. "Vampires have a high pain tolerance, have superior strength and reflexes and hearing, prefer the dark to the light, although it doesn't burn us as portrayed in movies and books." He put his arm into sunlight streaming through the balcony doors. "You see?" He set his arm down again at his side. "We can eat garlic, wear silver and worship at any church, and we live long, long lives. We're not immortal. We can die. It just takes a lot more to keep us dead."

"Sounds almost idyllic."

He turned his head and met her gaze. He wanted her to know that it was not as perfect as it seemed.

"The hardest part is seeing the people you've come to love die long before you'll ever see the inside of a grave. I have suffered many losses in my life. Love is not easy."

She reached across the sofa and touched his arm, squeezing it gently. "I'm sorry. I didn't realize how truly lonely that must be."

She released her hold and drew back her hand. Caine wanted to reach out, grasp it and set it back on his arm. A tingly sensation had started where she had touched him. He wanted that feeling to spread through his whole body.

"You never married?"

He turned his head and looked up at the ceiling, not wanting Eve to spy the pain in his eyes. "Once. Long ago."

Sensing he didn't want to discuss it, Eve remained silent. He wanted to thank her for that, but he too stayed quiet, words suddenly stuck in his throat. It had been over seventy years since the death of his wife, Amanda, but the pain still lingered inside, shielding his heart from all emotion. Closing his eyes, he sighed, not quite ready to release that barrier.

Beside him, he could feel Eve's uncertainty from his silence. He imagined that she was thinking hard about his reasons, deducing all manner of motives. Regret washed over him that he couldn't yet give them to her.

Turning his head, he opened his eyes and looked at her. She, too, had her head resting on the back of the sofa, and her eyes were closed. Her face was serene; the lines usually furrowing her brow were gone. He watched the slow rise and fall of her chest, battling the urge to touch her there. To feel the steady rhythm of her heart.

Her lips twitched at the sides. Could she feel him staring at her? "I'm not sleeping. I just want to rest my eyes a moment."

"Okay," he answered.

"Will you talk to me, so I don't drift off?"

"About what?"

"I don't know. How about the lab? Tell me how you became the chief."

He smiled, realizing it was so like Eve to want to know about the lab, about work, rather than ask about something personal. In the short time he'd known her, he'd found that she was very career driven, she lived the job.

Just as he did.

"I became chief because no one else wanted to," he started. "I guess it came from necessity at first. We needed a lab, I had the money to fund it, then the mistress asked me if I wanted a job."

She chuckled at that. "Really? I think you're making that up."

"It's the truth." He smiled to himself.

She laughed. It was a deep sexy giggle that had his blood pumping. He knew she wasn't trying to entice him, but that was exactly what was happening. He turned his head and looked up at the ceiling again, willing away the thoughts that invaded his mind.

"Tell me about the baron. What's up between you two?"

"Ah, yes, Laal Bask. Well, what can I say about him that would not include insults?" he remarked, wanting to hear her laugh again. "He thinks I want his job. Which I don't. I'm not a politician. I don't think I would work with Mistress Ankara very well. She's worse than he is. Ambitious as hell and manipulative. She'd sell her soul for a higher position in politics. I wouldn't be surprised if she's schmoozing with your Captain Morales in hopes she can somehow gain some clout with human politicians." He turned toward her again and his voice faded off.

She was sound asleep.

His lips twitched as he watched her. She looked so peaceful, like an angel. Reaching across the sofa, he captured a stray strand of silky hair in his fingers. He loved the feel of it against his skin. So soft, so sleek. He brushed it from her brow. She stirred under his brief touch and he wondered how she would react if he touched her again, in lower, more intimate places.

Gritting his teeth, he snatched his hand back and let it fall at his side. He had better stop thinking of her in those terms. It was stupid and dangerous. Nothing good could come of it. Didn't he already learn that lesson once long ago?

Closing his eyes, he tried to still his mind and relax. But it was impossible, not with Eve just a few feet away, her tantalizing scent clouding his mind and boiling his blood. His body hardened at the thought of her soft and pliant, open to him.

In his mind, he saw her naked and writhing on the sofa, her legs spread wide inviting him to taste, to take. He wanted to. More than he wanted to take in his next breath, he wanted to devour her, to possess her completely. The thought of her long shapely legs wrapped around his waist as he thrust into her slick core nearly drove him mad. He had to bite down on his tongue to stop himself from fulfilling his fantasies. The metallic tang of blood filled his mouth.

Opening his eyes, he stared down at his clenched hands. They itched to reach over and touch her. To run his fingertips over her warm bare skin and brand her as his own. Gritting his teeth again, he stood up. He needed to get out of the room before he did something they'd both regret.

He couldn't be held accountable for his thoughts, but he was for his actions. He had come too far with his training to throw it away in a moment of weakness.

Although for Eve, for this woman, it might be worth it.

Reaching down, he had to touch her face one more time. Trailing a finger over her cheek, he rubbed it across her lips until they parted in an unconscious sigh. Oh, how he wished for that sound in his ear as he coaxed it from her with the press of his fingers on her body, at her center. How wet would she be for him?

Cursing, he pulled his hand away, but couldn't seem to move from his spot. He stared down at her. She was too much of a temptation. He couldn't resist her any longer.

Chapter 18

Take me. I'm yours.

Sighing, Eve opened her arms and enveloped Caine, pulling him tight to her body. His heat seared her even through her clothing. Or was it that she was burning from the inside out? Raging with desire, she couldn't tell where one heated sensation started and where the other ended. Was it him, or her? Together they were a raging inferno.

Parting her lips, she invited him to kiss her. She wanted to experience the same intensity she had that night in the alley. And she didn't want it to stop this time. There was nothing blocking them. No one interrupting, no one watching. It was just him and her, alone together. Even if only for a few hours, they could finally let down their guards and revel in the powerful feelings that had constantly swirled around them since the moment they'd met.

He found her mouth, sliding his tongue over her lips and between them. Darting in and out playfully, he taunted and teased them both with his tongue and teeth and nipping at her bottom lip. She loved the feel of his lips on hers, and the way he growled low under his breath when he swept his tongue over hers and she reciprocated in kind.

She wondered what it would take to make him growl out loud, like an animal.

She could feel his restraint bubbling just under the surface of his desire. She knew he held back. That he pulled himself away from doing and taking what he truly wanted. And she wished he'd let go. She wanted to scream to him that she would not break, that she was strong enough to handle it.

But when she stared up into the bright beam of his eyes, and felt the muscles in his arms and legs quiver with barely controlled hunger, she couldn't be too sure. Sometimes, he looked like a man just scarcely holding onto his humanity.

Her hands raced over him, searching. She needed to touch him, to feel the heat of his body beneath her palms. Her fingers played over the buttons of his dress shirt. One by one, she popped them open, unconcerned with whether they broke off or not. Finally, she was able to part the cotton and streak her hands over his chest. His skin was soft and smooth. But hard as granite underneath.

Playing the tips of her fingers over his nipples, she reveled in the way he gasped and groaned into her mouth. She swallowed them down while she continued to run her hands over his muscles and rake her nails over her skin.

With his hands in her hair, he tilted her head up and nibbled on her chin. She loved the way his fangs scraped her skin. Shivers of excitement rushed through her as she pondered the reasons why. It was like flirting with danger, dangling a string in front of a cat, standing on a ledge with a thirty-foot drop and no rope to speak of. She didn't really want him to bite her, at least not consciously. But there was definitely a subconscious thrill to know that he could.

She had read that a vampire bite could be euphoric, sending the person into a state of rapturous pleasure beyond imagination. Was she brave enough to suggest it? Would he bow to her request?

Tingles of desire raced over her as his lips traveled lower, his tongue trailing circles over her throat. He gently bit at her, teasing. But when he glanced up into her eyes, she could see what he was asking, what he wanted, and he wasn't playing.

Swallowing down the urge to gasp, Eve ran her hands up and down his body, her fingers finding the button of his trousers. As she undid it, Caine nipped at her neck again. His fangs raked over her skin.

This time she did gasp as waves of lush pleasure lapped at her. An ache, deep and intense, throbbed at her center. There was only one thing that could ease her torment. Only one thing she wanted, more than anything before. Caine. She wanted, needed him deep inside her. Only then could she ease the ache of her body, heart and soul.

Surrender was only seconds away. She was his completely.

When she glanced down at him, she saw that he was already naked, the hard length of him was full and arched toward her. When had she stripped him of his clothes? Looking down at herself, she too was completely unclothed. Had she blacked out?

She could feel the sofa at her back as Caine pressed down on her. Her legs were spread around him. She didn't remember doing that. In her fervor, did she lose sight of herself? Heat spread over her like a flash fire. Her breath was coming fast, too fast. She could barely take in air.

Caine's fingers found their way down her belly, over the mound of her sex and into her slick folds. Arching her back, she moaned when he slid his fingers into her, testing her, teasing her sensitive nerves.

It was too fast. She wanted to slow down. Panic surged through her as he bit at her throat again. Did she really want this? She had no idea what would happen if he bit her. She hadn't read anywhere how vampires turned their victims, or even if they could. She'd just read how blissful their bite could be.

Writhing underneath him, Eve tried to push him up, but he was too strong, too involved in what he was doing to respond to her nudges. With bile starting to rise in her throat, she tried again to push him up off her. Instead, he grabbed her arm and held her still, nuzzling harder at her throat.

"Caine," she panted. "Please."

He must have misinterpreted what she was asking for as he nibbled harder on her skin. The plea in her voice must have sounded like desire and not rising panic.

"Stop. I don't want you to bite me."

"Don't be afraid, Eve. It will only hurt for a minute," he breathed, his voice thick with arousal.

She shook her head, and shoved at him. "I don't want it, Caine. Please don't."

But her words were cut off when he plunged into her simultaneously between her legs and at her throat.

A sensation she'd never experienced before exploded through her. A delicious mixture of pain and pleasure seared her flesh, and her mind. She suddenly went deaf and blind to everything around her. The only thing she could discern was a loud rushing sound like water surging over a fall.

It was her blood pumping through her body. And filling the mouth of her lover…

Gasping, Eve jerked out of her sleep. Her heart was racing like a jackhammer. She put a hand to her chest. It had all been a dream…

Sitting up, she glanced around her. Caine slept only a foot away from her on the sofa. She sighed, and dropped her head back onto the cushions. It had seemed so real. Pain still ticked at her throat, like someone had snapped her with an elastic band. And a deep throb pulsed between her legs.

She brought her hand up to her neck and tried to rub away the sensation. It tingled over her skin, but it wasn't all that unpleasant. None of it was. And that was what scared her the most.

Fear swirled around her, but despite it all, she still wanted Caine, and everything that came with him.

After taking a few deep breaths, her heart slowed. She closed her eyes again, and tried to relax. She still had a case to solve. Maybe if she concentrated strictly on that she could forget about the emotion swirling inside her. She wouldn't do anyone any good if she was unfocused.

Being around Caine was becoming dangerous. She wanted him with a desperate heart, but knew it would do neither of them any good. They were too different. They had completely separate destinies. Their lives could never come together. She was foolish to think otherwise.

It was just too damn bad that being foolish could feel so damn good.

Chapter 19

The high-pitched clamor of his beeper jolted Caine awake. Yawning, he sat up, dug into his pocket for it, looked at the number on the digital display and swore under his breath.

Another dead body.

Stretching out his arms, his hand brushed against warm smooth skin. It was then he realized that he was curled up next to Eve on the sofa in her hotel room.

The last thing he could remember was feeling out of control and restless. He had left the room, hadn't he?

Glancing around, he spied an empty plastic blood bottle, a small one that a vampire could easily buy in a vending machine. He must've left the hotel room, wandered down the hall to the utility room and bought a bottle hoping it would soothe his caged beast.

As Eve still had her clothes on, he assumed it must've worked.

He had dreamed of her, though. An intense vision of making love to her. Even now the tips of his fingers tingled with the memory of her skin. How soft and pliant she had been under his body.

He hadn't meant to enchant her, to project their love-making into her mind. It was something vampires did to seduce their potential mates or victims. The lock on his desire must be tentative at best if he was projecting without a concious decision to do so.

Thankfully, she had stopped him before he could bite her. That would be something he couldn't take back. It would be the first step in turning, and that was the last thing he ever wanted to do.

Before he could move, her eyes fluttered open and she yawned. Realizing his close proximity, her cheeks flushed a bright pink.

Pushing to his feet, Caine smoothed down the wrinkles in his pants, and cleared his throat. "We have another DB."

"How long were we asleep?"

Caine glanced at his watch. "About five hours."

Eve rubbed her hands over her face, and then pushed to her feet, avoiding looking directly at him. "Well, at least we ate."

Caine smiled as he surveyed the two room service carts. They had managed to eat most of what was on the trays. "That we did."

Avoiding his gaze, Eve padded across the room and grabbed her purse. "Are we ready to roll?" She continued to the door and opened it.

He hesitated, feeling like he should say something, anything, to defuse the tension in the air. However, he couldn't think of the right words. Everything that came to mind would be inappropriate and only cause more problems. Therefore, without anything further to say, Caine nodded and followed her out of the room.

By the time they reached Darkfall Avenue and Main Street, there was a small crowd gathering behind the yellow perimeter tape. Caine parked along the street behind a police cruiser. They jumped out of the vehicle, grabbed their kits, flashed badges to the officers standing at the yellow tape and wandered down the alley toward the area where Mahina and a few other officers waited.

"Nice day for a dead body." Mahina smiled but there was no humor in her expression. Sunglasses shielded her eyes, but Caine didn't need to see them to know that this body was a whole lot different from their usual DBs.

On the ground next to a large green Dumpster, Givon crouched beside a naked form.

Caine approached him cautiously, his eyes downcast on the cement looking for anything out of the ordinary. When he was next to Givon, he stopped, set his kit down and surveyed the situation.

"Lividity is fixed. Rigor has come and gone. Liver temp normal, and you got some bug activity." Givon stood and jotted his notes in his book. "So, I'd say he's been dead over twenty-four hours."

"Thanks, Sil."

The coroner nodded, and then said without humor, "Have fun."

He brushed past Eve as she sidled up next to Caine, setting her own kit next to his. Caine heard her intake of air.

"Where's his head?"

"That's a good question," he answered, glancing around the area near the body.

Crouching down next to the body, Eve started her evidence collection. "There's a lot of transfer on this body."

Mahina stood at the victim's feet. "He was found in the Dumpster."

"Oh, great," Eve commented, as she went into her kit and came away with a camera. She started taking pictures of the body.

Caine motioned toward the two officers standing over a derelict slumped on the ground, his hands cuffed behind his back. "Is he a suspect?"

"Officers found him chewing on the body. He claims he found it in the Dumpster then dragged it out to chow down."

"He doesn't look strong enough to drag a dead body."

"He's a lycan. They found him in wolf form."

"Ah." Caine nodded. Lycans were extremely strong. Some stronger than the average vampire. Long ago, he had a tussle with one and barely defeated him. Caine still had the scars on his back to prove it.

He glanced back down at the body then up at Mahina. "Monty's on shift now. Why did I get the call?"

Mahina handed him a clear plastic evidence bag. He took it and sighed. Sealed inside was a Crimson Strain poster.

"I found it near the body, under the Dumpster. I don't believe in coincidences. Do you?"

"No, not particularly. Thanks for catching this."

"That's what I do. Catch things."

"Do you think it's one of the band members?" Eve asked as she scraped under the victim's fingernails into a paper collection envelope.

"We won't know until we get the corpse back to the lab and run fingerprints. Until then, we process this like every other body, with care and precision."

"I'll have a little chat with our suspect at the station," Mahina said, nodding to where the filthy bum sat shivering.

"I don't think he's our killer, but he might've seen something." Trying not to breathe in the rotting odor from the trash bin, Caine looked down at Eve while she processed the body, bagging every fiber and item still clinging to his skin. "We're going to need his head."

Glancing up at him, she quirked one brow. "Where do you think it is?"

Caine motioned toward the green trash bin.

Eve stood and put a hand on her cocked hip. "Who's going in?"

Mahina smirked. "Better let the boss do it. It's much too messy in there for—"

"I'll go in," Eve blurted out.

"No, it's all right, Eve. I think it's best I do it."

She blinked at him several times, and he could see a twitch in her cheek. Waves of hostility rolled over him. It tasted like licorice on his lips. *Interesting.* He rather enjoyed the flavor.

"You don't think I can handle going into a Dumpster to do my job?"

"I didn't say that," he protested.

From beside him, Mahina smirked again. "I think you put your foot in it, Valorian."

Eve turned on her. "And you can put your foot in it, too, Captain Garner." She stripped off her gloves, shoved them in her pants pocket, picked up her kit and started back to the vehicle. "I'm going to go put overalls on, then I'm going in the Dumpster to find the damn head."

She pushed past them both with an indignant sniff of her nose and lift of her chin.

Caine turned and watched her march down the alley.

"She's got spunk. For a human," Mahina commented.

Caine nodded, trying to hide his amused smile. "I've been noticing."

The horrid smell of rotting food and unmentionable garbage nearly did Eve in as she tossed another black plastic bag out of the trash bin to Caine.

For the past hour, she'd been methodically chucking

out complete bags of garbage for Caine to inspect, while she dug deeper into the bin looking for anything resembling a head. So far, she'd come across several fish heads, and a decomposed cat, but no human head.

Sweat dripped down her forehead and from under her ponytail, ran past the collar of her blue overalls and down her back. Careful not to rub her face with the soiled latex gloves she had on, Eve dabbed at her face with the sleeve of her uniform. She was definitely going to need a shower. Probably two of them.

She was regretting opening her big mouth—once again—and landing herself in a situation she was not able to deal with. Digging around in rotting waste was not likely the best way to prove herself to Caine. He probably wouldn't have thought any less of her if she had refused to go in. However, she would have.

"Any luck?" Caine popped his head up over the rim of the trash bin.

Startled, Eve stumbled. Tripping on a broken wooden chair leg, she fell backward. She twisted in the air, putting her hands out to break her fall and ended up on her stomach, face-to-face with a waxy, pale visage. The crowning piece from their dead body.

Sucking in air like a fish out of water, she scrambled to her knees to get away from the decomposing head of their murder victim.

Stretching out with his hand, Caine tried to reach her. "Eve, are you all right?"

Swallowing the rising bile in her throat, Eve nodded. "I believe I found what we were looking for."

"Can you grab it and hand it to me?"

"Yeah, give me minute." Licking her lips to stifle the gag reflex, Eve shuffled closer to the head. Carefully, she removed the trash surrounding it. Once the surroundings were pushed back from it, she took hold of a hunk of black hair and gently pulled it out of its snug resting place.

Bits of paper, cloth and other debris stuck to the gory neck wound. It almost looked like streamers hanging down from a hot air balloon. That was if the balloon had split lips, sharp fangs and a bullet hole in its forehead.

Trying not to look at it, Eve stood and handed it off to Caine. She set it in his hands then eagerly grabbed the edge of the green bin so she could get out. But she found that she was in too deep. She couldn't lift herself out.

Again, she hooked her hands over the rim and tried to push her body, scrambling against the metal side of the bin. She was too tired, or too weak, to be successful. Defeated, she dropped back down and let out an angry huff.

"Need some help?" She heard Caine's soft chuckle as he appeared above the rim again, and he offered her his hands. "I'll pull you out."

With an angry glare, she took his hands and allowed him to pull her up so she could swing her leg over the edge. Once she had her right leg over, she yanked her hands from under his and dropped to the ground. Unfortunately, the motion made her slip forward and she banged her knee on the metal bin when she landed.

Caine was there again, reaching out to her,

touching her shoulder. Not that she didn't want him to touch her. She did, desperately. But she didn't want him to think she *needed* him to. She wanted him to believe that she was a strong, independent woman. Not some whiny, hopeless person who had to have a man tend to all her problems.

She knocked his hand away. "I'm fine."

"It's all right to ask for help, Eve."

Stripping her gloves off, she pushed back the hair sticking to her sweaty face. "I'm not an invalid, you know. You don't have to treat me like I'm so fragile," she huffed. "I'm a strong person. I *can* do this job. Even in *this* city."

"Okay," he said staring at her.

"Would you have stopped Lyra from jumping in that Dumpster?"

"No."

"Then why me?"

He opened his mouth to speak, but obviously thought better of it and stopped. Licking his lips, he sighed. "It won't happen again. You're right. You've proven yourself. You don't need me to protect you." Reaching down, he picked up the head encased in plastic and tucked it under his arm. "From now on, I'll treat you like the rest of the team. No special treatment."

Nodding, she wiped her face again. "Good."

Caine started back down the alley to the vehicle. "Could you grab my kit? My hands are full," he tossed over his shoulder while he kept walking.

Eve glanced down at the two metal suitcases on

the ground. Sometimes, she had trouble carrying her own. Sighing, she gripped each handle and hefted the kits. They were heavy, and she found her shoulders pulled as she walked.

Well, she did say she didn't want to be coddled. Maybe she should've waited until after they were back at the lab before she made that statement.

Chapter 20

"Well, he was definitely shot and his head was cut off postmortem."

Caine resisted the urge to berate Givon, especially when Eve was standing right next to him, looking eagerly up at the M.E. "I figured that out, Sil. Now give me something that's going to help."

"He was shot at close range." Givon pointed to the stippling, which resembled a bunch of small reddish-black spots on the victim's forehead. "Between six inches and two feet. So maybe your vic knew the shooter." Reaching behind him, he grabbed a small gray plastic tray. He handed it to Caine. "Here's your bullet. Pulled it out of his frontal lobe. Small caliber bullet with a low velocity."

Caine picked up the fragmented bullet and tossed it into an evidence bag. He'd take it to Kellen to see if it matched anything they had on file.

"The wound tracks on his neck indicate a large blade at least seven inches, with a serrated edge. Whoever did it was very strong and likely sliced through his neck in a matter of seconds. There were no hesitation marks or chopping wounds." He made his hand into a flat edge and brought it down toward the victim's neck. "He set it against the neck, and pushed down in one or two fluid motions."

"Same knife as with Lillian Crawford?"

Givon nodded. "Could be. Can't say for sure, but definitely similar. I'll make a mold of the wound to compare."

"What about the bite marks?"

Givon pointed to the torn flesh on the body's side and thighs. "Postmortem. I'd say the lycan came across a hearty meal and couldn't resist. Took chunks out of the meatiest parts."

Caine nodded in agreement. That's exactly what he had thought. The bum had likely been looking for food scraps when he went Dumpster diving. Surprised by a fresh dead body in his trash bin, it was likely too enticing, especially for a lycan who had been starving.

He'd let Mahina know their findings, and get her to release the bum in the morning. He'd make sure that in lockup the man received a meal at least.

"Anything else?"

"He was a young vampire. I'd say he was no older

than one hundred. In relatively good shape, except for the small holes in his arm." He lifted up the body's left arm and pointed to a clump of pinpricks on the inside of his elbow, a perfect spot for injecting substances into the veins.

"A drug abuser?" Caine asked.

"Possibly. I sent a sample of his blood to tox."

"Okay. Thanks, Sil." Caine patted his friend on the shoulder before he walked out of the autopsy room.

"Oh yeah, I got the word on that bone you found."

Caine stopped and turned around.

Givon handed him the bone in a clear plastic evidence bag. "It's *Sus domesticus.*"

Taking the bag, Caine stared down into the bag. "It's a pig bone?"

Givon nodded.

"Okay. Thanks." Perplexed, Caine continued out of the autopsy room. Eve followed him close behind, her eyes dancing with eagerness above the green surgical mask.

Once they were outside the swinging metal doors, Eve whipped off her mask and her green cloth wraparound gown. "Do you think this new vic is one of our guys?"

After removing his own mask and gown, he frowned. "Maybe. We'll hit up Gwen to see if she's made a match yet." He marched down the long hall toward the elevator to the second floor. "I don't want to make assumptions. They can only get us into trouble."

"I know, but I can feel it in my bones."

He nodded. "If it is one of our guys, then the other is tying up some loose ends."

The elevator doors opened, and they went in. Eve pushed the button to the lab. And as the doors shut, Caine could sense her excitement at nearing a solution to the crime. He too felt elation at having a lead. He just hoped it led them in a straight line and not around in circles.

The minute the doors slid open and they stepped out onto the floor, Lyra zipped down the corridor toward them, a piece of paper in her hand, and a sparkle in her eyes.

"We got a hit on AFIS." She handed the sheet of paper to Caine while she rattled off the information on it. "Jamie Duncan, arrested for drunk and disorderly. Guess where?"

"The Howler?" Eve guessed.

Lyra smiled at her. "Good guess."

"Do we have an address?" Caine asked, as they continued to walk down the hall toward the lab.

"Apartment six, 1016 Twelfth Street."

Stopping right at the door to Gwen's lab, Caine gave the sheet back to Lyra. "Good work. Where's Jace?"

"He's out tracking down possible van matches with Detective Calder."

"Okay, call Jace and get him to meet us at that address." Caine handed her the other evidence bag with the pig bone in it. "Log this, too. It's a pig bone found under the bed at the last crime scene."

Lyra nodded, and raced off down the hallway the opposite way from where they had come.

Caine and Eve stepped into the lab. Gwen looked up from her microscope and motioned toward the printer. "Your results."

Moving to the printer, he slid the paper from the tray and glanced down at it. Eve was right beside him, eyes alight, peering over his arm at the paper. "He's a match to one of our perps."

"Yup."

"Thanks for the quick work, Gwen."

She waved at him while still looking into her microscope. He knew that was her signal for "you're welcome, now get the hell out of my lab since I'm really busy."

As Caine exited the lab, Eve met him stride for stride. He glanced over at her as they marched down the hall toward the firearms department. She looked like a kid right before a big game, the most important game of the season.

She met his gaze. "We're close, so damn close. Can you feel it?"

He nodded. "We'll get Kellen to run the bullet, maybe we'll get a hit, and then we'll head over to our new vic's apartment. Hopefully, we'll find something there to lead us to his killer and our second perp."

"I love this part of the job." She laughed. "Right before you put all the pieces together and solve the puzzle. It's a rush, isn't it?"

He grinned at her enthusiasm. He really liked that about her. Her passion for the job. Passion. Something they deeply shared.

Could they share it on another level?

Before he could respond with something he probably shouldn't say, his cell phone shrilled from his pocket. Digging it out, he flipped it open and put it to his ear. "Valorian." After a few moments, he flipped the phone closed and slid it back into his pocket.

"Is there a problem?" Eve asked, worry furrowing her brow.

"Politics." He sighed. "I have to meet the baron in my office."

"I can take the bullet to run ballistics."

"Are you sure?"

She nodded. "I'm part of the team right? I can do this on my own. You can trust me." She put out her hand for the evidence bag.

He set the small paper envelope into her palm, closing his hand around hers. "I do trust you, Eve. It's Kellen I don't trust."

She laughed but didn't pull away from his touch. "He doesn't scare me."

"Well, he scares me," he stated with a chuckle.

"At first he was a little hard to take, but now that I'm used to y'all, it's a walk in the park."

After a final squeeze of her hand, Caine pulled his away. The sudden loss of the warmth that had been spreading up his arm surprised him. He hadn't been totally aware of the sensation until it was taken away. Was her touch really so potent? He wondered what would happen if they increased that connection, touching other, more intimate places.

Again, thoughts of her writhing underneath him flashed in his mind.

Aware that she was staring at him, a little flush in her cheeks, Caine cleared his throat and smoothed a hand down his tie. Did she feel the sensations, too? How could she not when they seemed to crackle all around them like lightning?

"Okay, I'll meet up with you later."

She nodded and turned to continue down the hall toward the firearms room. He watched her walk, enjoying the way her trousers fit over her shapely rear end. It was becoming increasingly hard to keep his desire in check. He found the more he was around her, the more he wanted to be with her. Professional distance was becoming a thing of the past.

He knew she was attracted to him. He could smell it on her, taste it in the air whenever they were together and feel it sizzle on his skin. And it was more than just a physical connection. She was definitely beautiful, with a body that made a man wonder what she would look like spread out on his bed, with only the moonlight casting beams on her flesh, waiting for him to enter her.

Pinching the bridge of his nose where a headache brewed, Caine turned and made his way to his office where the baron was likely waiting. His thoughts were for nothing. There was no way they could consummate their feelings for each other. It was unethical and dangerous.

A vampire's lust was overpowering. Eve would not be able to handle his desire. It would overwhelm her and consume her until she could think of nothing else but him. Even after, she would desire him like no other. She would be branded with their lovemaking, his scent so ingrained into her skin that the craving could drive her mad.

He wouldn't let what had happened to Amanda, his late wife, happen to Eve. Morally, he couldn't venture down that path once more.

When he'd fallen in love and married Amanda, he had made a fatal error. He had tried to turn her. She hadn't been strong enough to survive the transformation. Her heart had stopped beating and he didn't have the power to get it going again. He had killed her with his selfish desire to possess her for an eternity.

He vowed never to make that mistake again.

"I knew you were coming," Kellen announced the moment Eve stepped through the door.

Taken back, she halted at the door and almost considered turning around and leaving. "Ah, do you have psychic ability or something else that I should know about?"

Grinning like a lunatic, he shook his head. "Nah, I could smell your perfume floating down the hall."

She should've felt some sense of relief from his statement, but it just made her more nervous. He made her nervous. For the past few days, he'd been around every corner watching her, eyeing her as if she were his next snack.

He neared her and lifted his nose in the air taking in a deep whiff. "You smell intoxicating."

"Um…"

"But you know that already, don't you? I'm sure the chief must tell you that all the time."

Taking a step back, she thrust out her hand, showing him the little evidence envelope. "Can you check out this bullet, please?"

"Sure." He took the envelope from her and rounded the large rectangular counter to stand near his microscope and computer. As he dumped the bullet onto the table, he glanced up at her and winked. "Good job changing the subject."

Refusing to acknowledge his remark, Eve came around the counter to stand beside him. Not right beside him, but near enough that she could watch what he was doing. "Is it a twenty-two?"

Kellen picked up the bullet with tweezers and set it in a small vise under his microscope. After setting the tweezers down, he peered into the lens, adjusting the magnification.

"It's a thirty-eight, darling." He glanced sideways at her. "Do you want to look?"

She nodded, and then looked through the microscope after he took a few steps back.

"See those striations there? Those are unique to the gun this came from, a Smith & Wesson .38 Special, or possibly a .357 Magnum. Find me the weapon and I'll get you a match."

When she raised her head from the lens, Eve was very aware of Kellen's presence. He hovered over her. She could feel the heat from his buff body.

"My God, I can see why he wants you."

She whirled around and glared at him. "Excuse me?"

"Caine." Smiling, Kellen boxed her in against the counter, putting an arm on either side of her. "I can completely understand why he wants to possess you." He leaned toward her and sucked in a deep breath through open lips. His eyes nearly rolled back in their sockets. "You are an exquisite piece of ass."

"I suggest you back away from me." She tried to control the quaver in her voice, but she heard it, as she was sure did he.

His eyes seemed to glow from the inside as he spoke. "I'm surprised he hasn't taken you yet, but it's just a matter of time. I can sense his intent from all the way down the hall. He hasn't been frequenting the Club to slake his desires, so he must be suffering something fierce."

Pushing away from the counter and breaking his hold on her, Eve shivered and started for the door, eager to get out of the room. "I don't know what you're rambling about."

"Sure you do, love. But I won't tell anyone." He put his finger to his lips. "Your secret is safe with me." He laughed. "I'm good at keeping secrets. I know everyone's. Including Caine's. Including yours."

Eve didn't stay to ask what he meant by his last comment. She wanted nothing more than to get out of that room and away from Kellen. He made her extremely uncomfortable. She believed he had meant to do exactly that.

Was it that obvious that she found Caine attractive? That there was something brewing between them? Could everyone see it as clearly as Kellen had? God, she hoped not. The last thing she needed was for the rumors to start flying about her again.

Because of her foolhardy relationship decisions, her career had suffered before. Her affinity for powerful men in charge was well known. Captain Morales had reprimanded her once before. He had kept it out of her record, but he warned her if anything like that were to happen again, he would dismiss her.

Stopping to lean against the wall, Eve closed her eyes and took in a few deep breaths. She needed to get ahold of herself. Kellen had purposefully unnerved her, she knew, but if she was going to face Caine again, she had to be cool and calm. He could sense her emotions. She didn't want him to know how confused she truly was.

And the last thing she was going to do was go running to him with tales of sexual assault by one of his team members. Kellen was a vampire. Maybe that was how he was with all women. She had no way of knowing. And that angered her. She was still running around the lab blind, with no sense of how or why things worked the way they did. It was just another glaring reason why her being here was a dangerous idea.

Sighing, she pushed away from the wall, walked two feet and went into the women's washroom. She needed to get herself together.

At the sink, she turned on the cold-water tap and leaned down into the basin. She splashed her skin, hoping the iciness would snap her out of her shock and start to put the pieces of her mind back together. She wouldn't be any good to this case with her brain scattered and unfocused.

"God help me," she muttered.

One of the toilet stall doors crashed open, and Lyra marched out, sidling up to Eve at the next sink to turn on the tap.

"Are you all right?" she asked while she washed her hands.

Nodding, Eve shut off the cold-water tap, turned and pulled a few paper towels off to wipe her hands and face dry. "I'm good."

"Are you sure?" Lyra eyed her as she too wiped her hands dry. "I know I'm not the most approachable person, but sometimes I do listen."

Eve smiled, but shook her head. "I'm good."

"Okay." Lyra tossed the paper towel in the trash and went to walk out. "Tell Caine that I'm following a lead into the dark arts, and I'll call him if I come up with anything."

Eve nodded, but then took in a deep breath, letting herself trust this woman. "Has Kellen ever given you any trouble?"

"As a witch or as a woman?"

"Either. Both."

Lyra scrunched her face as if thinking of just the right thing to say. "Don't let him bother you, Eve. He likes to rile things up. He likes to disturb others, plain and simple. Most of what comes out of his mouth is bull." She smiled. "Disregard everything personal he had to say. He did it to upset you. And by the looks of you, I'd say it worked." Lyra rummaged around in her small black bag and came away with a small spray bottle. "Here." She handed it to Eve. "This will help."

"What is it?"

"Just a little something I whipped up. Helps distress and boosts energy. And if you've been crying, takes the red out of your eyes and the bags out from under them." She waved a hand in front of her face. "Just like magic."

Smiling, Eve took the bottle and popped the top off it, smelling it. It had a light floral scent, jasmine perhaps. "Thanks."

Lyra nodded, then grabbed the door handle and opened it to step through. Eve heard her mutter under her breath, "I know she is, Gran, but you can't force people to talk, you know."

Eve held the spray up to her face, closed her eyes and pushed. A light mist floated over her head. Instantly she felt better. Her muscles loosened and she almost felt giddy.

Capping the bottle, Eve slid the spray into her purse. Hmm, magic indeed.

Taking in another breath, Eve tucked a stray hair behind her ear, smoothed down the line of her pants and raised her chin. She could project an air of professionalism. She could make everyone see a strong, confident woman. She'd been doing it for years.

The last thing anyone needed to know, especially Caine, was that Eve was scared. Scared of messing up this case, scared of failing on this assignment and deathly scared of falling in love with her boss.

Maybe two out of three wasn't bad?

Chapter 21

"Did Lyra say she couldn't get ahold of Jace?" Caine asked Eve as he maneuvered the SUV onto the curb in front of a rundown apartment complex on Twelfth Street.

"Yes. No answer on his cell phone," she responded from the passenger seat.

Caine glanced out his side window and spied Jace pacing the sidewalk on the opposite side of the street. "Hmm, either our lycan friend is psychic or he's one step ahead of us."

After parking, Caine slid out of the vehicle, grabbed his kit from the back and hustled across the street to where Jace, along with another detective, Ren Calder, impatiently tapped his foot next to a dirty, rusted-out white van. Eve trailed behind.

"Okay, how did you end up here?"

Jace showed him a piece of paper with vehicle information on it: *White 1989 Chevy van, registered to Jamie Duncan, apartment 16, 1016 Twelfth Street.*

"Well, Jamie Duncan is now our second murder victim this week." Caine handed back the paper to Jace. He reached toward the detective, and they shook hands. "Good to see you, Ren."

"You, too."

After that formality, Caine proceeded to walk up the sidewalk to the apartment complex door. He pressed the bell to the landlord's apartment.

A few moments later, a gravelly female voice sounded on the intercom. "What?"

"I'm Caine Valorian with the crime lab. I have a warrant to search apartment sixteen, belonging to Jamie Duncan."

The door buzzed open. Caine grabbed it to hold it open, and then turned back to Jace. "You and Eve take the van, Ren and I will do the apartment."

"What? No way," Jace protested, his eyes narrowing to deadly slits.

Caine set his steely gaze on Jace. "Don't even try to go there, Jericho. I've had more than enough of your attitude this week." Jace started to open his mouth, but Caine wasn't through talking. "One more complaint from you, and I'll take you off this case. You'll be sitting at the lab going over surveillance video from the Griffin High School graffiti case."

"I hope she's worth it," Jace muttered before turning and storming back down the walkway to the van, his hands clenched into tight fists.

Lifting a brow, Ren brushed past Caine into the apartment complex lobby. "I'll just go and talk to the landlady and get the legal end of things taken care of."

Still holding the door open, Caine took in a breath, prepared for Eve's tirade about working with Jace and how rude he was. It didn't come as he expected. Instead, she looked relieved.

Since she'd come back from the firearms department, she had been acting differently. Something had happened, but she refused to talk about it, claiming that Kellen had been a perfect gentleman and a professional. After she had said that, he knew she was lying. He didn't even need to smell it on her. But he had, and it smelled like vinegar.

He hadn't had time to speak with Kellen before they left to come to this address, but when they returned to the lab, the two of them were going to have a long conversation. Out of all his team members, Kellen worried him the most. He was fun loving and eccentric, seemingly always looking for a good time, but underneath that façade, Caine knew that Kellen was as unpredictable as a tornado.

And for humans who didn't understand vampire physiology, that tornado could rip apart any sense of reality.

"Are you all right?"

She nodded. "Fine."

He grabbed her arm before she could turn to go

back down the walkway. "I know that you aren't, Eve. I can sense your uneasiness around me, that's why I paired you with Jace. But I thought we were past that. I thought—"

She pulled away from his touch. "And so does everyone else." She raised her chin and met his gaze. "I don't need any rumors flying around about us. Let's just work this case and be done with it. Then we can both go back to our normal lives."

Before he could respond, she turned and walked down the stone path to where Jace had already popped open the side door of the van and was waiting, not very patiently, for her.

Caine hated to admit it, but her rejection stung. Although he knew she was right, Caine didn't want to just work the case and be done with it. He wanted more. For himself and from her.

It was certainly a blow to his male ego that she pulled away from him so easily, just as they were starting to connect on a physical level, but he knew deep down inside that this was the best for them both. She was just a stronger being for breaking the ties first.

Caine knew from painful experience that vampires and humans couldn't mix. It was too difficult, too painful for both parties. It was best that they both walked away before anything more serious could transpire between them—or before it became impossible to part.

That still didn't stop him from bending the metal handle on the door before he walked through and let it swing shut behind him.

* * *

Jace grunted at her when Eve made it down the walkway to the van. Ignoring him, she snapped on her latex gloves, flicked on her flashlight and went to work inside the vehicle. Maybe if she let her job consume her attention, she could stop thinking about Caine, and how much she wished they could be together.

On her first initial sweep, she noticed a few things—first, a burgundy rug. On visual inspection it seemed to match the carpet fibers from the first crime scene. Secondly, there was electronic equipment piled in the corner of the van. Things like guitar amps and cords could make a match to the copper wire they had. And finally, she noticed that Jamie Duncan didn't take care of his possessions very well. The van had papers, cigarette butts and other items strewn about the interior of the vehicle. It was going to make for interesting evidence collection.

Glancing over her shoulder, she glared at Jace who was still standing outside the van, his arms crossed, and looking surly. "Are you going to do some work, or pout all day?"

"I'm not pouting."

She smirked. "Huh, tell that to your bottom lip." Eve opened her kit, took out a few collection bags and began to pluck carpet fibers and cigarette butts with her tweezers.

As she did that, Jace finally burst into action and started taking multiple photos of the rug, contents and console of the van.

When he was done, she opened the passenger door and climbed into the seat. She popped open the glove compartment and went through its contents. The only things of interest were a couple of pay stubs from a place called Shadowwood Studios.

A recording studio? It would make sense if he were connected to the band Crimson Strain. Maybe he was their roadie. And just maybe he was at the concert in San Antonio that Lillian Crawford had attended.

"Look what I found," Eve said, swiveling around to show Jace the pay stubs.

Taking them, he nodded. "Well, that would make sense of this sticker." He swept his flashlight over one of the amps in the back. A white and black frayed sticker was on the side. *Property of Shadowwood Studios.*

"I bet that's where our Crimson Strain boys record," Jace added.

Nodding, Eve slid the pay stubs into an evidence bag and looked around the front console. It was dirty with smudged fingerprints all over it. Maybe too many prints. "There are a lot of prints here. Maybe we should take it back to the lab and superglue it."

"Good idea," Jace commented as he jumped out of the van. "I'll radio Caine and let him know what we found and see if we can get over to Shadowwood to ask some questions."

While Jace radioed Caine, Eve resisted the urge to smile. She breathed a sigh of relief that Jace was actually working *with* her and not trying to push her out of the case. She knew they would never be friends, or even friendly, but she felt like she'd just passed some kind of milestone.

She also felt like they were making advancements in the case. The sensation that they were getting close to the answers hummed all around her. She loved the rush of that. It was just one of the many reasons she became a crime scene investigator. That and the sense of danger connected to working a scene.

Of course, while working in Necropolis, the danger was exponentially multiplied by a thousand. Working around Caine, even more so. She didn't feel threatened by outside forces when she was with him. No, she knew she was physically safe from harm. It was from inside she sensed the danger. The danger of losing herself completely to him.

Every time she was close to him, tingles of anticipation crept over her. The anticipation of fulfilling desire and ending her longing for him. Two things that had gnawed their way into her heart since meeting him.

Waking up next to Caine on the sofa in her hotel room didn't help matters any. It just intensified her feelings for him. The fact that he didn't push her, when he knew damn well she was vulnerable and could've easily been persuaded into anything, made her feelings for him even stronger. And she knew it was more than the lure of his vampiric charms that called to her. He was much more than the sum of his vampire physiology. He had soul and character far deeper than she could've ever imagined. She wanted to know him, all of him, with every passing moment.

The end of this case couldn't come soon enough.

She didn't know how much more she could withstand. It helped that she was physically away from Caine, forced to think of other things, but she knew the moment she saw him again, the intense need and desire to make love with the vampire would wash over her once more.

She guessed the trick was not to be alone with him.

She would do her job, work the case and stay as far away from him as possible.

Jace popped his head back into the vehicle, the radio clamped in his hand. "Meet Caine at the doors. You can ride over to the studios with him, while I take the van back to the lab."

She opened her mouth to respond, but Jace had already left.

Damn it! Just when she was starting to believe her own words.

Chapter 22

Shadowwood Studios was on the corner of Shadowwood Avenue and First Street, and very near to both
murder sites. Caine made a note of that. It could be
just a coincidence, but he didn't believe that; he
believed in the evidence. And it was currently pointing to the studio.

As he pulled up to the curb in front of the studio,
he glanced over at Eve. She was in the passenger seat,
seat belt on, hands firmly planted in her lap. She
didn't look up, although he knew she could sense his
eyes on her.

When they had exited Jamie Duncan's apartment
complex, Eve had been waiting at the front door for
them. He'd felt that she was distancing herself from

him. It was like ice on his tongue. Without looking at him, she said she would meet him in the SUV, and then proceeded to walk toward the vehicle.

He knew why she was behaving this way, knew it was the logical thing to do, but he hated it. He despised not being able to talk plainly with her, not be able to share a look or a thought without realizing that it would do nothing but damage them in the end.

He parked and turned off the vehicle, Detective Calder pulling up behind them. "Okay, let's go. Hopefully someone will tell us something we need to know to catch this guy."

The moment Caine, Ren and Eve stepped through the door to Shadowwood Studios, Caine recognized the haunting sounds emanating from the recording room. There was no mistaking his favorite chanteuse's evocative voice.

Caine glanced over at Eve. Her brow was wrinkled, and her jaw clenched. He imagined she was trying very hard not to let the emotion of Nadja's song overwhelm her. At this close proximity, even Caine was finding it difficult not to be carried away.

Before they could move any farther into the studio, a security guard met them. Caine knew he was a lycan. The guard was huge, but for a man his size, he still managed to move with speed and grace. Most lycans had that uncanny poise.

"Can I help you?"

Ren held up his badge. "N.P.D. We're here investigating the murder of Jamie Duncan. We understand he worked here."

The guard nodded, his eyes wide, the news obviously surprising him. "He does…did."

"What's your name?" Caine asked.

"Lucas Marchak."

"Did you know the deceased, Lucas?"

"Yes, but not well. He was into, um, other stuff."

"Like?" Caine urged.

"Drugs and partying all the time."

Caine continued. "Did he party with the members of Crimson Strain? They record here, don't they?"

Licking his lips, Lucas shuffled his feet. "I should go get the manager."

"Okay, Lucas. Is it all right if we watch the recording?"

"Sure," the guard said, moving to catch up with Caine as he walked through an open doorway and into the recording studio. Stopping just inside the doorway, Caine stared, transfixed, into the glassed booth.

Nadja Devanshi was everything Caine expected her to be. Tall and willowy, cascading ebony hair sweeping around her tiny waist and a pale oval face highlighting impossibly green eyes and a lush red mouth. An ethereal enchantress.

Yet, Caine's blood didn't boil at the sight of her. In fact, his pulse had not jumped at all. It was not the reaction he was expecting when faced with this vampiress, a woman he had dreamed of one day meeting.

He suspected the young human woman sidling up to him at the studio window was the reason for his odd non-reaction. She had her hands over her ears, and tears streaming down her face.

Lucas the security guard waved at Nadja through the glass.

Eyes glinting like wet emeralds, she put her hand to her neck and made a cutting motion. Instantly the orchestra accompaniment switched off. The echo of her clear, poignant voice reverberated around them, nearly making Caine cringe. The high note was like an ice pick in his brain.

Strange. He never heard that kind of sound before in her music. Was that what Eve felt listening to the songs, a sort of sweetly piercing pain? Had he been deaf to it all this time?

Nadja moved through the room, opened the door and swept into the studio. Caine couldn't describe the way she moved in any other way. It seemed that her feet didn't even touch the ground. Was she floating? A vampire had to possess a lot of power to perform that kind of feat. Even Mistress Ankara didn't hold that kind of power, and she was close to one thousand years old.

Smiling, she extended her hand to Caine. "Caine Valorian, how lovely to finally meet you."

He took her long elegant hand in his, surprise lifting his brow. "I wasn't aware that we knew each other, Ms. Devanshi."

"Reputation only, I'm afraid."

He withdrew his hand and had the urge to rub it against his leg. Tingles of something not quite pleasant radiated over his skin. She was throwing off a lot of energy, and he wanted to know why.

"I didn't realize I had a reputation."

She laughed, the sound almost brittle, like icicles. "Oh, don't be modest, Caine. All powerful vampires have reputations to uphold. You're no different." Her gaze swept over the other people in the room, then landed on Eve and stayed there. Smiling, she tilted her head as if studying something fascinating. "And you bring a human. How interesting. Is she a gift?"

Caine could sense Eve mentally backing away. She didn't physically move, but she was shrinking inward from Nadja. He wondered how much power she could feel coming from the chanteuse, and how much longer she could handle it.

"We're investigating the death of Jamie Duncan," he said.

Her severely plucked brow lifted. "Jamie's dead? I wondered why he never showed up for work today."

"He worked for you?"

"Well, yes, I do own the studio."

"Do the members of Crimson Strain record here?"

"They do. Are my boys in trouble?"

Eve sniffed. "Your boys? Are you their mother?"

Caine could feel the temperature in the room drastically lower the minute Eve's words were out of her mouth. He should've warned her about a vampire's temper. If he had known they would be talking to Nadja Devanshi about the murders, he would've left Eve at the lab. He didn't know for sure, but he gauged her age at close to two thousand years old. This lithe creature held more power in her pinky than most of the vampires in Necropolis banded together.

"You could say that." Nadja smiled. "I discovered

them and helped them make their first CD. They're lovely boys."

Taking a step forward, Eve said, "One of your lovely boys—"

Caine set his hand on Eve's shoulder and stopped her from advancing. "The boys are in jail pending charges. It seems they had a little road trip into San Antonio. Xavier is up on assault and we also believe that he may be linked to another murder."

"Your human is a tad unruly, Caine. You should keep her on a tighter leash."

"Tighter leash?" Eve clenched her hands into fists.

Caine grabbed her arm and kept her from speaking. "I apologize, Nadja. She is not used to the rules and regulations in our city. I'll explain them to her."

Smiling, Nadja waved her hand in dismissal. "You do that, Caine."

"My colleague, Detective Calder, can continue with some more questions if that's all right?"

"Certainly. I have nothing to hide."

Still holding Eve by the arm, Caine marched out of the recording studio, through the antechamber and out the door into the night air.

Spinning her around, he set Eve up against the wall and leaned into her, his eyes glowing. "What are you doing?"

"She insulted me."

"I warned you about vampire politics. I told you not to open your mouth no matter what. You could've jeopardized the case with your antics."

"My antics?" Eve growled. "That woman is—"

"That woman is nearly two thousand years old and has more power than the entire U.S. Army. With a single thought, she could've had you on your knees begging her for whatever she wanted you to."

Sighing, Eve lowered her chin. "I'm sorry."

Caine swiveled around and looked up at the night sky. "No, I'm sorry. I was kidding myself thinking that you could handle this." He turned on his heel and looked down at her. "This is my fault, okay? I'm going to have Ren take you back to the lab, or to your hotel, or whichever."

She pushed off the wall, and met his gaze. "You can't do that. The baron said I was to be active in this case."

"I don't care what he said. You're in danger on this case. I won't jeopardize you any longer." He hated having to do this to her. He knew how much she wanted to be involved in the case. It tore him inside to see the dejected and hurt look on her face. However, she didn't understand how incredibly close she came to being injured, severely injured.

Caine could feel the anger building inside Nadja. It was like acid against his skin. And if he could feel such pain from her thoughts, he could only imagine the agony Eve would've endured if Nadja had released that energy onto her. She wouldn't have survived the assault.

Eve had no clue what he had saved her from. To know would only drive her insane with fear. He'd keep it to himself and hope she got angry enough with him that she stayed away. Far, far away from this part of the case.

"You can't push me out when we're so close to the truth, Caine. I think I earned the right to be here. It's not fair."

"I don't care about fair right now. All I care about is solving this case. And it can't be done when I'm constantly worrying about you." He didn't mean for it to come out like it did. He didn't want it to sound as though she was being punished. But in the end, she was being punished because of his inability to keep her safe.

The sparkle in her eyes faded. Replacing it was a pain he never wanted to see there. Pain he never wanted to put there. But he had.

It was foolish to think that she could handle being on the front line on this case. He supposed he had allowed it to happen because of his own selfish need to be with her, to be around her. His unchecked hunger to consume her, his predatory instincts to protect her, had almost put this case in jeopardy. Something he had never done before.

Maybe it was for the best. If she were furious with him, then she would be more careful. She would re-inforce her guard and maintain a distance. He could keep her safe the further away from the case she got.

Gathering his anger and fear, he pushed away from her, and dropped his hands to his sides. What he really wanted to do was gather her in his arms and soothe the hurt, the pain that he had just inflicted on her. But he couldn't. This was something they both had to endure so Eve would stay safe.

Lifting her chin, she met his gaze. "You know

you come across as someone that's all about justice, and righting the wrongs of society. But all you care about is how *your* case is run, how *your* case is handled, how it will look for *your* team when it's solved." She took a bold step forward, her eyes sparking with fury. "You don't care about Lillian Crawford. You don't care about the pain and suffering she must have felt when she bled out in that dirty hotel room, alone and unable to defend herself from monsters she thought only existed in nightmares." Hair fell over her forehead, and she swiped at it furiously. "Everything I've read about your race is true. You're all coldhearted, selfish and egotistical. The only reason you're a crime scene investigator is because you like the power of it." She shook her head, and turned so her back was all he saw. "I was so wrong about you."

His heart shattered as her words sunk in. Emotional pain he hadn't felt in years ripped through him like a jagged knife, shredding his soul into ribbons. Swallowing, he let out a breath and clenched his hands into tight fists.

He wanted nothing more than to convince her she was wrong about him. Wrong about his motives, wrong about his feelings. However, to do so would be futile. She wouldn't believe him. He had proved everything she had said with his actions.

He could do nothing but accept her words and bite back his urge to prove her wrong. To prove he was a good man.

Taking the SUV keys from his pocket, Caine

pressed the unlocking mechanism. The vehicle beeped and the doors unlocked. He walked to the back door, and opened it for her.

"I'll get Ren and he can take you wherever you want to go."

Without a word, Eve brushed past him and jumped into the vehicle. He shut the door and pressed the locking button. Through the tinted window, he could see her head hanging, and almost felt her ragged intake of breath. She looked like she was on the verge of crying. And there was nothing he could do about it.

Feeling impotent and unworthy, he turned and went back into the studio to get Ren and try to continue with the case. If nothing else, he could get them one step closer to solving it, and be one step closer to getting Eve out of the city and safely back into her own world.

In time, she would forget about him. Move on with her life, solve other cases and experience other lovers.

Although deep down inside, he hoped she would suffer in emotional purgatory as long as he knew he would.

Chapter 23

The odor of her ire combined with her terror was like ambrosia to his senses. A heady mixture that nearly had his eyes rolling back in his head.

From his perch in the shadows of the alley across the street, he had been witness to Caine's and the woman's argument. *Eve…* that was her name. An appropriate one, he thought considering what he had devised for her.

He thought it must be fate that had brought her to Necropolis. Instead of having to hunt in the human city for a human woman, the perfect one had already volunteered to come, all on her own. *What a brave specimen.*

And the time was coming for his plan to be

executed. A little sooner than he had wanted, but circumstances seemed to be changing.

Caine and his team were proving to be more astute than he had previously deduced. He hated underestimating people, but it was possible he had with this vampire. He seemed to be working against his own nature to solve this case. This was disconcerting, but interesting.

He wasn't worried though. No one, not even the notorious Caine Valorian, could stop him. He'd been planning and devising this for far too long to be stopped now. Nothing but his own death could halt the future. Even then, he knew another would pick up his cause and continue.

This event was bigger than all of the players put together. Bigger than anything anyone had ever witnessed. And he was going to be right at the center of it.

As was she.

Watching as Caine slammed the door and went back into the recording studio, his hands itched to have her, to touch her. It was not time yet, but he wanted her now. Licking his lips, the thought of what he could do with her before the right time made his blood roar and his cock twitch. Thinking about the delicious torments he could perform on her had his hands shaking and his heart pumping.

He couldn't wait any longer. He had to possess her now.

Before he could step out into the street, the door to the studio opened, and the lycan cop walked out.

Rage surged over him as he watched Detective Calder open the SUV door, collect Eve, put her in his car, start the vehicle and drive away.

Leaning against the wall, his breath coming in hard, raspy pants, he closed his eyes and focused on the future. He would have his way soon. A few more days and he would be able to fulfill all his dark fantasies with the woman.

And while he was doing so his fate would be fulfilled and he would become the most powerful being ever to walk the earth.

Chapter 24

Anger fueled her movements as Eve flipped through the evidence logs, tossing crime scene photos and reports onto the rectangular tabletop in the analysis room. The employee list from Shadowwood Studios, courtesy of Detective Calder before he left the studio, was what she'd been staring at for the past half hour.

Ever since she directed Ren to drive her back to the lab, she'd been holed up in the room going over all the evidence they had. If Caine was going to keep her out of the field, she would solve the damn case right here in the lab. He couldn't stop her from thinking.

She was holding on to her anger, allowing it to dictate her actions, because the alternative was too damn painful. Caine had hurt her with his words.

He had cut to her core and flayed her to the bone.
After the closeness she was starting to feel from
him, his betrayal hurt even more. She had mis-
judged him, misunderstood the feelings she thought
he had for her, and that had cost her more than she
wanted to admit.

Therefore, instead of wallowing in her pain, she
wrapped her anger around her like a shield. She was
guarded now, steel-fortified, and no one, especially
Caine Valorian, was going to get behind her de-
fenses again.

Flipping to another crime scene photo, Eve
wondered if Caine was still at Shadowwood
Studios talking with his special friend, Nadja. She
hated to admit it, but jealousy also fueled her anger
and hurt. She'd seen the way Caine had looked at
the singer.

Certainly, she was gorgeous and elegant, and had a
voice like an angel, but Eve had redeeming qualities,
too. She wasn't as spit and polished as Nadja, but she
was pretty when she wanted. Hadn't Caine looked at
her with desire during that evening in her hotel room?

Maybe *she* should've let him know that she was
interested. Because she had a sneaky suspicion she
wasn't going to get another chance to be with him
again. And however career crushing it would be, she
yearned for it like a lovesick puppy.

Lyra popped her head in the door, startling Eve
from her reverie. "Where's Caine?"

"Talking with his girlfriend," Eve grumbled under
her breath.

"Did you just say he was talking to his girlfriend?" Lyra asked as she stepped into the room, a lopsided grin on her petite face.

Eve smirked. "No."

"Okay, do you know where he really is?"

"I'm right here." They both jumped when Caine seemed to materialize in the doorway. "What's up?"

"I got a name from my contact down in the Sticks. Someone has been asking a lot of questions about demonology and summoning. A vampire."

Eve leaned forward in her chair and at the exact moment that Caine spoke she asked, "What's the name?"

Caine glanced down at her, and she thought she saw a twitch at his lips. Her treacherous heart jumped at the possibility of it turning into a smile.

"Melvin Howard. Around six feet tall, short-cropped blond hair, blue eyes."

"Are you sure?" Caine asked.

Something in Eve's mind flashed back. She knew that name from somewhere. Glancing down at the table, she spied the employee list for Shadowwood.

"Mel Howard is a paramedic out of Silent Hill," Caine said. "I know the guy."

"He's also an employee of Shadowwood." Eve handed Caine the paper.

As Caine read over the list, adrenaline shot through Eve's body. This was it, she could feel it. They had their killer.

"Could this be our guy?" Lyra asked. "Maybe it's a coincidence."

"I don't believe in coincidences. That would explain one of the reasons he was at the Red Express."

Eve perked up. "Oh my God, he was there that night we—" She could feel her cheeks blush even as the first word was out of her mouth. Coughing into her hand, she tried to disguise it as something other than embarrassment. "—picked up Xavier."

"Yes, he was, and conveniently missed treating Xavier in the back of Mahina's car."

"It would explain the heparin in Lillian's system," Eve offered, the thrill of the catch thrumming through her body. She was on the edge of her seat.

"It sure would." He lifted his gaze and met hers. A zing of energy bolted through the space between them. He was as excited as she was about finally catching a break and solving the case. It wasn't airtight yet, but Eve had a feeling it was damn close.

She wondered if Caine experienced this kind of connection with all his crime scene team members. Deep in her heart, she hoped not. She hoped that this, whatever it was, was just between the two of them. It would be something she could take home with her when she left. Something she could remember about him and their almost relationship.

"I'll call Mahina. Tell her we're picking him up." Caine flipped open his phone and dialed.

"I'm going to find Jace and tell him to meet us in the garage. I don't think anyone wants to miss it when we catch this guy."

Lyra flashed Eve a grin, then marched out of the analysis room, leaving Eve and Caine alone. After finishing his call to Mahina, he slid the phone into his pants pocket, and turned to look down at her.

Suddenly nervous, Eve shuffled the crime scene photos and reports into a nice, neat pile on the table. In the midst of possibly finding their killer, she'd forgotten that she was furious with Caine. Now other emotions, stronger, more intense feelings were surfacing and she didn't know what to do with them.

"Eve, I want to apologize."

"No need," she said as she scooped up the papers and shoved them back into the case file folder.

His hand covered hers on the table. "There is a need."

Looking up she met and kept his gaze. The air seemed to sizzle between them. A warm sensation flowed over her skin from where he touched her. Despite her anger toward him, she desperately wanted that feeling to spread over her entire body. It felt too damn good. He felt too damn good.

"I was completely out of line. You have earned your place in this lab. And I appreciate all that you've contributed to the case."

"Thank you," she said and smiled. Elation filled her. He did care about her. She could see it in his eyes. Maybe they could somehow make something work between them. A night, a week. She didn't care. Was it so impossible?

"I just wanted you to know that before you went back to your own lab. I'll make sure to tell your captain."

Her elation faded and ended up as a hard lump in

the pit of her stomach. She'd been wrong. All the man wanted was to get rid of her.

Pulling her hand out from his, she pushed to her feet, and handed him the case file. "Right. Then let's get it over with, shall we? Maybe I can be back home before the sun rises."

Brushing past him and out the door, she hurried down the corridor before he could see how upset she was. She could feel Caine walking behind her but she never turned around. She refused to let him know how he had hurt her again. It was humiliating that he had seen her cry and felt the need to apologize to her. He'd told her before that he wasn't used to someone with so many emotions. He had been so right.

Chapter 25

Caine stood beside Mahina, adrenaline racing through his system as she pressed the doorbell of Mel Howard's quaint little bungalow at three o'clock Sunday morning. Eve and Lyra stood huddled together on the sidewalk, both with their kits, in front of the house while Jace and Ren were at the back.

He worried a little about Eve being on the scene. Hadn't he left her defenseless one too many times before? Fighting back his nervousness about Eve's vulnerability, Caine told himself to keep calm. Eve was with Lyra. She was safe. The whole team was here.

He felt they deserved to be present when they seized the perp. Or the alleged perp in the eyes of the law. But in Caine's mind, Mel was guilty as hell. After going over all the evidence, he was one hundred percent sure the vampire was their serial murderer. Not only did he have the means, they also discovered that Mel Howard had a .38 registered to him. Therefore, the whole team was wearing Kevlar vests.

Mahina pressed the buzzer again. Putting his ear to the door, Caine could hear the doorbell echo inside, but he didn't hear anything else. Maybe Mel wasn't home. He wasn't working. Caine had already called to see if he was on shift.

Mahina picked up her radio and pressed the button. "We're going in. On five."

As she picked up the battering ram, she nodded to Caine and counted. "One, two, three, four, five."

On five, she swung the thick black metal cylinder at the door. The wood on the frame splintered and the door slammed open. With her gun drawn, Mahina rushed in, Caine following close behind.

"Police!"

Caine heard the back door crash open, and Ren's twin announcement of arrival. "Police!"

Caine did a quick survey of the living room. A lamp in the corner was still on. A half-full glass of blood sat on the glass coffee table. And Caine could detect the odor of fear in the air.

Sidling up next to Mahina, he whispered in her ear, "He's here."

Nodding, she spoke quietly into her radio. "Be on alert. Suspect is still in the house." She glared at Caine. "And you, get behind me. Your head isn't bulletproof, you know."

He motioned for her to continue the search. As she

moved from the living room into the kitchen, he got behind her. She was right, his head wasn't bulletproof and he wasn't about to lose it. Not now, anyway.

The rest of the house was dark, but neither one of them needed a flashlight as they both possessed superior night vision. But so did their suspect.

A quick perusal of the kitchen showed dirty dishes in the sink and a leaky drip in the faucet, but nothing else. As they crept down the hall toward the bedrooms, the stink of panic invaded Caine's nostrils. Either Mel was in one of the bedrooms waiting for them, or he had recently just run down the corridor with thoughts of escape racing in his mind.

Mahina and Ren went down the hall first, their backs to the wall. Caine and Jace lagged a little behind. On Mahina's right, a door was ajar. Silently, she crept to it and peered in, gun pointed confidently. Glancing behind her, she shook her head indicating that it was clear.

Coming back into the hall, they continued inching their way along the wall. There were two bedrooms ahead, one on the left, and one on the right. Both doors were closed.

Taking in a deep whiff, Caine tried to determine what direction the odor was coming from. The smell was so cloying, seemingly coming from the walls themselves, that he couldn't tell.

Mahina and Ren looked at each other just as they neared the closed doors. A nod was all that was needed between them to know exactly what to do. They had been on a few busts together before.

On the count of three, Mahina and Ren kicked open the doors and charged into the bedrooms. Caine held back as they searched the rooms. Any minute, he expected to hear shouting or shooting. However, he heard nothing but Jace's ragged breathing as he pushed up behind him, eager to get in on the action.

After a few more minutes, Ren wandered out of the bedroom, empty-handed, and shrugged. "He ain't up here."

"There's a basement, maybe he's hiding there," Jace offered.

Caine shook his head. "He came this way. I'm positive."

Mahina poked her head out of the other room. "There's an open window."

"He escaped out the window," Jace said. "Which way do you think he'd run?"

A scream perforated the silence of the night, giving them their answer.

Eve!

Caine swung around and ran back down the hall toward the front door, his heart hammering in his chest. Thoughts of bloodshed already flashed in his mind. *Please, God, don't take her from me now!*

Eve didn't see him come around the corner until it was too late.

Before she could react, the suspect had knocked Lyra unconscious from behind with a blow to the head, and was quickly approaching Eve, his lips pulled back in a feral grin. Instincts kicking in, Eve held her ALS flashlight in her hand like a club, the light source on. If he was going to come at her, he was going to get an eyeful of ultraviolet and a knock in the face.

With every step back Eve took, he matched her. She knew he was mocking her, taunting her with the fact that he was so much stronger than she was. That at any time he could end this and kill her with a sweep of his hand and a bite of his teeth.

His contempt toward her made Eve angry. She was tired of being afraid. Wasn't she exactly as everyone saw her? A scared human woman thinking she could play with the creatures of the night. Well, she was damn tired of being afraid. She was just damn tired.

"You're going down for the murders, Mel. We have enough evidence to convict you and lock you up for life."

His steps faltered a little as she spoke. Eve thought he likely wasn't expecting her to talk to him, stand up to him. He expected her to cower and shrink. A fly to his deadly spider.

"Keep talking, human. I like to play with my food."

"Maybe if you give yourself up, they'll go easier on you."

Mel laughed. "Honey, I'm never going to see the inside of a prison cell. *He* won't let that happen."

He? Who was he? Was there someone else involved with the murders? Eve didn't have time to process that information. Mel leaped forward and pushed on her shoulders, shoving her to the ground. He loomed over her, his open mouth baring his fangs.

"Playtime is over. Time for the main course."

As he pressed down on her, one of his hands on her head slowly turning it to bare her neck, she swatted at him with her flashlight. She connected twice with the bridge of his nose before he grabbed her hand and pushed it up over her head. With tears running down his cheeks from the impact on his nose, he closed in on her neck, in no obvious pain.

Eve struggled and wriggled, trying to break his firm hold on her. She refused to be this guy's snack. She would not be a victim like Lillian Crawford had been.

"I bet you're going to taste better than the girl. I wish I could screw you first."

"Not before I screw you," Eve grunted as she brought her knee up right between the suspect's legs.

He might be a vampire, but the guy still had the usual equipment. By the tortured look on his face, Eve had landed a direct hit.

Grunting, Mel released his hold on her head and brought his hand up to his crotch. While he was pre-occupied thinking about the pain, Eve kneed him again and twisted her body to push him off. The move worked and she was able to roll away from him. However, as she pushed to her knees, he was on her again, grabbing her by the hair and pressing her into the cement face-first.

Her cheek scraped against the asphalt as he pushed on her head. She clamped her eyes shut when she felt hot air on the side of her neck. Holding her breath, she waited for the sharp pinch of his teeth on her flesh.

As random thoughts crossed her mind in the

moment of panic, images of Caine dominated her vision. Where was he? Hadn't he heard her scream? She didn't want to die without telling him how she felt. How she wanted him. How she'd never met someone she respected and admired as much as she did him. That she saw past the vampire and glimpsed the real man inside. A man she wanted to know and possibly love.

The first pinch of pain seared through her as he sliced her skin with his fangs. A warm rivulet of blood ran down her neck to drip on the pavement beneath her. She sucked in a ragged breath expecting the next onslaught of agony.

But it didn't come. Not for her anyway.

Before she could blink, Mel tumbled off her body. Shuddering from the rush of adrenaline, Eve managed to lift her head to see what was happening.

A few feet away, Caine and Mel wrestled on the ground. It proved to be a short battle with Caine on top. He sat on the other vampire's chest and punched him in the face several times fast. So quick Eve barely saw his arm move. But glancing at Mel's bloodied nose and lips, there was no doubt that Caine had landed several solid blows. The blood staining Caine's shirt proved that Mel had inflicted his own injuries, too.

Caine raised his arm again, but Mahina was there restraining him.

"That's enough, Caine. You made your point."

Shrugging off Mahina's hold, Caine stood and took a step away from Mel's writhing form. He

turned toward Eve and she gasped in shock. His face
was contorted in rage. Even in the dark, she could
feel the menace of his gaze. It was like looking into
the dark pit of something she didn't want to name.
She knew the menacing look wasn't meant for her,
that he had saved her life, but she couldn't stop the
shivers of dread from racking her body.

Taking in a ragged breath, she tried to push up.
Detective Calder was next to her, grabbing her arm
and helping Eve to her feet.

"Are you okay? Anything broken?" Ren asked as
he searched Eve's face and body for serious wounds.

Lifting her hand, Eve touched the side of her neck.
Her fingers came away tacky with blood. But it didn't
feel like she was bleeding any longer.

Ren must have noticed the look of horror on her
face. "He didn't pierce your artery. Just nicked the
skin. Don't worry, you won't be growing fangs
anytime soon."

Sirens pierced the early morning air. An ambulance and a police cruiser raced up the road toward
the scene. Ren held Eve's arm and directed her
toward the approaching ambulance.

"Let's get you looked at."

"What about Lyra?" Eve asked, suddenly remembering Lyra's knock to the head.

"She's fine. Being looked after, too."

As they shuffled across the pavement, Eve
glanced over at Caine. He was watching her, his
hands still clenched into tight fists. Jace was at his
side, talking rapidly to him. But Caine never took his

eyes away from her, as if Jace was not there. The dark look on his face was replaced with one of anguish and despair. Eve thought he looked so sad, tortured even, as if he had done something terrible, instead of saving her life.

Reaching to his side, she held her hand out to him as she passed. He lifted his arm toward her. Their fingers brushed against each other.

Eve felt the electricity sparking between them. The air suddenly filled with current and it all but sizzled over her flesh as the tips of their fingers touched. She wanted the sensation to last. Wanted to hold on to the way it tingled over her whole body.

But it soon passed as they were both ushered in separate directions to take care of their respective injuries.

Chapter 26

"What you have on my client is tentative at best, Captain Garner," the hawklike lawyer rattled off as he fidgeted in his seat next to Mel Howard in the interrogation room.

Caine watched through the two-way glass as Mahina smiled her I-got-you-by-the-balls smile and slid a piece of paper across the table toward the lawyer. It was the lab results on Mel's DNA. It matched what they had found on Lillian Crawford. Mel had had sex with her and had bitten her on the neck.

While the lawyer looked over the results, Mel stared straight ahead toward the mirror. He had a little smirk on his beat-up face. As Caine eyed Mel's injuries, his only regret was that he hadn't finished the job. For the first time in a long time, he had felt the urge to destroy another being. Remembering what Mel had done to Eve made him shudder with fury all over again.

Caine risked a glance to the side at Eve. She stood on the other side of Lyra, her hands clasped tightly together, watching the interrogation. He wondered how she was feeling, if seeing the suspect made her afraid or angry. He had a desperate urge to soothe her. To walk over to her, wrap her in his arms and never let go. However, as the case was nearly closed, the thought was futile. She'd be going home by dinnertime.

He turned back to the room and watched as Mel's lawyer fidgeted even more in his seat. "This just proves that my client had sex with the victim and took blood. Neither is illegal. It doesn't prove he killed her."

With a lift of her brow, Mahina slid a sealed evidence bag across the table. Inside was the knife Caine had found in the closet of the suspect's bedroom when they did a thorough search of his residence after Mel had been handcuffed and taken away.

"This is the knife we found in your client's bedroom, with the victim's blood on it." She pointed to another sealed evidence bag with a .38 Smith & Wesson inside. Jace had found the gun in the garage, in the suspect's vehicle. "This is the gun that killed Jamie Duncan. Ballistics matched the bullet pulled from Jamie Duncan's head. Your client's buddy and co-accomplice in the Lillian Crawford murder." Pausing, she cocked her head. "Should I go on, counselor?"

The lawyer glanced sideways at his client. Mel hadn't as much as flinched since being in the room. It was almost as if he was in some sort of trance.

Looking back down at his briefcase, the lawyer grabbed the handle and stood. "I guess there's nothing left to talk about. We'll see you in court."

"Yes, you will," Mahina said as she gathered the evidence together.

"You can't stop it."

Everyone in the observation room flinched away from the window when Mel spoke, the sound so deep, so menacing, that to Caine it didn't seem like his voice at all.

Mahina instinctively raised her hand to her belt, very near to where her gun was holstered. "What's that, Mel?"

Mel smiled and sprang forward in his chair as if on a wire coil. "It's already begun. He's coming."

Lyra glanced at Caine, a look of horror on the witch's face. "He's talking about Balam."

Caine shook his head. "It's just a ploy, Lyra. The guy's trying to rattle some cages. He knows he's going down for a long time."

"Who's coming?" Mahina asked.

Mel stood and leaned over the table, leering at the mirrored window. "He's coming for you, sweet thing. He's already had a taste of your blood, and he likes it."

Gasping, Eve turned from the window with her hand on her bandaged neck. Caine sensed the room filling with fear. Eve's fear.

Mahina motioned to the guard in the room. "Get him out of here."

The guard made a grab for Mel, but he danced out of the way and ran at the window. He smashed into it, opening up fresh wounds on his face. Blood splattered across the glass and ran down in thin lines.

"I can smell you, sweet thing! I can feel your fear!"

Caine crossed the room in two strides, gathering Eve in his arms. She didn't resist, but grabbed on to him in desperation.

"We got him, Eve. He can't hurt you."

While he stroked her hair and rocked her gently, two guards dragged Mel out of the room. Mahina followed them out. Jace and Lyra huddled together in the corner and remained in respectful silence as Caine comforted Eve.

She didn't cry, but he could feel her whole body vibrate with trepidation. He wished he could take it away from her. Take away the attack. But he couldn't. It was his fault she'd been attacked. He shouldn't have left her with Lyra. He should've stayed with her, or kept her with him. But he had been afraid of seeing her hurt. But in the end, she had been injured regardless.

He had failed to keep her safe.

The door to the small room opened and Mahina ambled in. She peered around at their faces. "Why so grim? We got the bastard on two counts of murder one. The Crimson boys are all facing charges of federal trespassing. We've done one hell of a job."

Clearing her throat, Eve pushed out of Caine's

embrace. She took a deep breath and smoothed down the wrinkles on her blouse.

"You're not worried over his outburst, I hope." Mahina eyed Eve. "Girl, he's so full of crap my eyes were watering from the stink."

Jace burst out laughing first. Then Lyra. Caine glanced at Eve and he saw her lips twitch. She looked up and caught his gaze. They both started laughing at the same time. When the five of them were finished laughing, Caine's stomach hurt from the effort.

Sobering, he looked at each of his team members and nodded, thinking how great each and every one of them was. "Good work, everyone. This was definitely a team effort." His gaze lingered on Eve. "We did right by Lillian Crawford."

She smiled and nodded. "Yes, we did."

As everyone went around the room congratulating each other, Caine continued to watch Eve. She smiled when Lyra hugged her, and nodded politely when Mahina shook her hand. She was a strong woman, a lot stronger than she gave herself credit for. She thought she was weak for needing to be comforted, but she was so wrong. She was one of the strongest women he'd ever met.

She'd come to a foreign place without any knowledge of what she truly faced and dived in without complaint. She'd been attacked three times, faced danger and death, and still she charged forward. He admired that. Most people would tuck tail and run.

Jace came up to Caine and shook his hand. "Well,

Chief, I'm out of here. I'm going to go sleep for a week."

"I don't know about a week, but I'll give you two days."

Smiling, Jace clapped him on the shoulder. "I'll take it." He then turned toward Eve. "Have a safe trip back."

She gave him a half smile. "Thank you, I will."

After Jace left, Lyra approached Eve and hugged her again. "I'm not usually a touchy-feely person, but I felt like I needed to hug you again."

Eve chuckled. "Well, I appreciate it."

"Gran says to be safe."

"I plan on it."

After nodding to Caine, Lyra bounded out of the room. That left Mahina. With a hint of a smile on her face, she nodded to Caine, then Eve. With a salute, she was gone.

Now, they were alone, and the tension solidified.

Caine turned toward her and offered his hand. She took it.

They stood a foot apart, hands clasped, gazing into each other's eyes. Caine searched her face for a sign of her true feelings. He could sense confusion, desire and apprehension wafting off her.

For the past five days he'd pulled her in and pushed her away. Afraid for her, and afraid of her. He was as confused as she: about what happened between them, what hadn't and what they both wanted.

Eventually, she shied away and dropped her gaze, pulling her hand from his. "I'm packed already. My

suitcase is in the staff room. I don't have to go back
to the hotel."

"I talked to your captain, and told him what a
great job you did, and that you should be com-
mended. I also mentioned maybe a raise in your sal-
ary. You certainly earned it."

"Thank you." She pulled at the creases in her
blouse again, then stepped toward the door.

Caine stopped her with a hand on her arm. "Have
dinner with me," he blurted out, not letting her back
away from him. He could see the retreat in her eyes.
He'd never have this moment again, and he didn't
want to walk away from it knowing he could experience something magical with this woman.

"Caine, it's only two o'clock."

"Lunch then," he said with a smile.

"Why?"

Raising his hand, he captured one of her stray curls
in his fingers and tucked it behind her ear. "I want to
show you that not all vampires are like that. Bad, evil.
That vampires can show affection and...love."

A single tear trickled down her cheek. He wiped
it away with his thumb. That was all the answer he
needed.

"I know you're a good man, Caine. You don't need
to prove it to me." She grabbed his hand on her cheek
and squeezed it. "Give me another reason."

"Then because I want to."

She pursed her lips together, and then nodded.
"Good answer. Where are we going for lunch?"

"My place."

Chapter 27

Thrumming with nervous energy, Caine unlocked the door to his town house. Even his hand quivered a little. The ride over had been one of uncomfortable silence.

Standing aside, he let Eve enter first. Without looking at him, she stepped over the threshold and stood to the side of the door, as if she were frightened to go farther.

He could feel her nervousness like electricity over his skin. It brought the little hairs on his arms to attention. He liked that she was nervous, though, and not afraid. He didn't think he could handle that.

After he came in, he shut and locked the door. Eve jumped a little at the clicking sound of the lock.

Smiling, she put a hand to her chest as if trying to stop her heart from thudding so hard. He could hear it as plain as a hammer on a board.

He wanted to laugh at how they were both behaving like teenage virgins on their first night. He supposed in a way they were.

"Would you like something to drink?" he asked. He loosened his tie and slid it out from around his neck. As he walked past the sofa, he tossed it on the edge.

"Yes, that would be nice."

He gestured to the living room. "Please sit. Make yourself comfortable."

As he poured them wine at the bar, Eve moved into the room and sat primly on one side of the sofa. Caine watched her from the side of his eye as she glanced around the room, taking in everything, her hands clasped tightly in her lap.

He came back with glasses of wine, handed one to her and sat on the sofa near her, but not too close as to scare her.

Smiling, she took a sip of the wine. The taste must've surprised her, because her eyebrows went up. "Oh my, that's fantastic."

"It's a two-hundred-year-old bottle of King Louis the Fifteenth's favorite wine." Caine swirled the dark liquid in his glass, smiling, as Eve nearly choked on her next sip.

She wiped her mouth and set the glass down on the coffee table. "Did you know him?"

"Only in passing. We didn't run in the same circles, so to speak."

Chuckling, she looked around the room again. "You have a nice place here. Very neat."

"I like order."

Smiling coyly, she glanced at him under her lashes. "I noticed. Rules and regulations, too."

"Well, without them, there'd be chaos." Setting his glass beside hers on the table, he pushed to his feet. "Would you like a tour?" He held out his hand.

Nodding, she took it and allowed him to pull her to her feet. Keeping her hand, he wrapped it around his arm as he guided her through his town house.

He could feel her vibrate through the sleeve of his shirt. Her arousal, like fresh-cut flowers on a spring day, wafted up to him. His heart picked up a beat as he led her down the hall to his bedroom. Nerves still pulsed through his body, but he was done being afraid of his desire for her. He couldn't keep it in check any longer. He was through running from something he wanted so badly it tore at his soul.

As they stepped over the threshold of the last room, he said, "And this is my bedroom."

Her heartbeat increased, he could hear. He could see the arousal on her face, feel it in her hands and sense it all around him.

She pulled her hand from around his arm, and began to fidget with the buttons on her blouse. "Caine…"

Turning, he stood in front of her, close enough to hear her sharp intake of breath when he did. "Yes?" he responded, his voice laced with his growing desire.

"I thought we were going to eat?" she asked breathlessly.

He took a bold step forward, and grasped her hands. "We will." He brought her hands up to his mouth and pressed his lips to the back of each one. "Later."

"Caine, we can't."

Shaking his head, he spoke. "Let's forget about the rules and regulations, Eve. We've focused on the case long enough. I want you. You want me. Let's focus on that for a while."

She let out another ragged breath. "I'm so nervous. I've never been like this before. Not even my first time."

"I won't hurt you."

"I know."

With that, he couldn't hold back any longer. Dropping her hands, he wrapped one arm around her waist and pulled her to him, tight. She opened her mouth to gasp, and he took it without pause.

She tasted like mint and black currant from the wine. Her scent filled his nostrils. A smell he would always associate with her, with this moment. Sweeping his tongue over hers, he bit and suckled on her plump lips. Eager to sample more of her. Eager to take and taste.

Clenching her hands in his shirt, she kissed him back. Hard and fierce, desperate. When she moaned, he swallowed it down, fervent for everything she would give him, and everything she would take. She'd only but to ask, and he would give it to her without complaint.

Burying his hand in her hair, he pulled it from her ponytail and swept it over her shoulders and down her back. He loved the silky feel of it through his fingers. The finest fabrics would never feel as good.

Cupping the back of her head, he deepened the kiss and, squeezing her tight around the waist, he walked them back into the wall. Finally, she was in his arms. Willing, and open for him.

God, she was more than he deserved.

After one last delicious nibble on her bottom lip, Caine pressed kisses to her chin making his way down her throat. When he neared her bandages, she stiffened and took in a ragged breath.

"It's okay. I won't hurt you. I promise," he vowed, then trailed his tongue over her skin, careful not to touch the bandage. He made tiny circles around it, and then moved lower to her collarbone.

As he kissed her, she gasped and moaned. Licking his way across her neck, he reached the other side and gently bit on her flesh. Moaning, she twisted her hands in his shirt, pulling at the fabric.

He moved up the side of her neck, licked her lobe and whispered in her ear. "I've wanted to do this for a while now. You are so damn sexy."

Moving his hand down, he captured her breast in his palm. She was soft and supple, curvy. Beautiful and luscious. Her body made him ache in need. He wanted to look at her, take in every mound and curve.

Feast on her with his eyes.

Taking a step back, he circled his hands up around the collar of her shirt. Her eyes widened when she realized what he was about to do.

With one yank, he tore her cotton T-shirt in half.

Underneath the simple fabric she wore a lacy white bra that stole his breath. It was such a simple garment, but it made him harden even more to see the bronzed flesh of her breasts barely covered by the see-through material.

Gasping, Eve reached for him, wrapping a hand in his hair. "Oh God, Caine, I'm burning for you."

His restraint broke with her desperate plea.

Grasping the waistband of her trousers, he pulled them apart. The button popped off and landed on the rug. The zipper tore open. Without waiting, Caine pulled her pants down to the ankles and tore them away to toss to the side.

He looked down at her and groaned.

She stood there pressed against the wall, quivering with desire, in her bra and lacy panties. Her lips were agape, swollen from his rough kisses. Her eyes were wide, dark with the desire he could smell on her soft golden skin.

He could barely hold onto his sanity. Bloodlust bubbled inside like an angry mountain of lava. Her perfume permeated his senses. The sight of her quivering flesh made him hungry. He wanted to devour every inch of her until she begged him to stop or urged him to take her even further.

He slid a finger under the band of her panties, sliding it down into her soft folds. She was wet and hot, eager for him. He brought his finger up to his mouth and slid it in between his lips to savor her flavor. She was like churned honey on his tongue. A flavor so delectable he'd find the best foods bland compared to her.

She watched him and moaned slightly in a demand for more. When her lashes lowered, and she stared at him through the dark hoods, his beast growled and pounded at his head to let him loose.

He did.

Taking hold of the band of her panties, he tore them off with one violent pull of his arm.

"Oh God, Caine."

He dropped to his knees, and gripped her thigh in his hands, pushing her leg up and against the wall. She wrapped her hands in his hair to hold on. He didn't give her a chance to take a breath before he suckled between her legs without mercy.

Intense, unbridled heat radiated over Eve's flesh. Her entire body quivered from the inside out as Caine feasted on her. She'd never been this hot, this wanton before. It was as if his touch seared her. Inflamed every inch of her body. She wanted him to touch her everywhere, explore every slope and fold of her flesh. She'd never felt this type of passion before. One that overpowered her and made her weep with need.

Again he stroked between her legs, stopping at her most sensitive spot. She could hardly breathe as her belly flipped over and over, like a roller coaster, and the muscles in her thighs tightened. An explosive orgasm built like a raging inferno at her center. It wouldn't take much more to push her over into the blistering flames of total and complete rapture.

Gripping his hair for support, Eve looked down at Caine as he licked and suckled on her sex. Gone was

the uptight man that followed the rules. In his place
was a feral being intent on driving her mad with
desire. She'd unleashed something she was unsure if
she could handle. By the pleasure surging over her
body, she wouldn't mind the effort of trying.

As if sensing her need, Caine raised his head and
locked eyes with her. His eyes glowed a brilliant
blue. She'd never seen a color so radiant before. It
unnerved her and excited her at the same time.

"You taste so damn good," he growled, the tips of
his fangs evident between his glistening lips. Then
he went back down and settled his lips over her again,
suckling gently.

Sweat trickled down her back. Her thighs tightened with expectation. Gripping his hair tighter,
Eve bit down on her lip as she felt the beginning
flutters of orgasm.

Caine increased the pressure, teasing her sensitive
nerves, and that was all it took for her to come
crashing down.

Moaning, Eve banged her head against the wall,
and squeezed her eyes shut. She'd never experienced
a climax so intense, so violent. She could only feel
as wave after wave of ecstasy crashed over her.

Caine released his hold on her and stood.
Opening her eyes, she stared at him. His lips were
swollen and his eyes glowed like blue moonlight.
He was so incredibly beautiful. Hauntingly so. She
knew he would forever haunt her mind, body and
soul.

Without a word, Caine offered his hand. He didn't

need to speak. The way he looked at her, with naked desire in his face, spoke volumes.

Taking his hand, she allowed him to lead her to his bed where he promptly sat her on the edge. He took a step back and unbuttoned his shirt. She watched his fingers as they flicked open button by button. She wanted those fingers on her, in her. Anywhere and everywhere, she didn't care.

Once his shirt was undone, he shrugged it off. Underneath he was all hard planes and sleek muscles. His skin over his chest was smooth and un-blemished. A stripe of dark hair lined his sternum leading deliciously down to the band of his pants and beyond.

Noticing the direction of her gaze, Caine smiled then proceeded to undo his pants. He did it with slow deliberation, teasing her, making sure that Eve was watching every movement. She was watching; she couldn't take her eyes off him.

After he pulled down the zipper, he let his trousers fall. Underneath he wore blue boxer shorts. A slow smile curved his mouth as he hooked his thumbs in the band and slowly pulled them down. When they were at his ankles, he kicked out of them.

He stood before her naked. Gloriously and sinfully naked. She sent a little blessing up to the heavens for making such a specimen of pure male beauty. And that he was all hers, for a little while at least.

He took a step toward her. Reaching out, she grip-ped him around the hips and pulled him closer. With her gaze locked on his, she wrapped a hand around his long length. He was like velvet iron in her palm. Soft and hard at the same time.

While stroking him, she watched as he struggled with control. She adored the way he worried at his bottom lip with the tip of his fangs as she squeezed the tip of him, and then dragged her palm down to the base. The way his breath quickened and jolted when she repeated the movement again and again sent delicious shivers over her body.

"Damn it, woman! You're killing me."

Grinning up at him, she leaned forward. "Oh yeah, how's this for a long, slow death?" She wrapped her lips around him.

She stroked him with her mouth, employing both tongue and teeth to increase the enjoyment, the pleasure, the play. By the way he gripped her hair and the sudden gasps that exploded from him, she knew she was effective.

With a loud moan, Caine pulled her head back. "Too much. I want to come inside you."

After releasing her grip on him, she was pushed back onto the bed. Reaching down, he grabbed a leg in each hand and pulled her forward, pushing her knees apart. The movement spread her open and exposed. Heat flooded her body at the prospect of what Caine could do to her. She was defenseless against his strength. He was in complete control, and she loved every minute of it.

Inching his way in and then out of her, he taunted her mercilessly. She thought she'd go mad. Her entire body was slick with sweat, and she could hardly catch her breath as he tickled and teased. She felt just on the edge of a steep cliff with every intent to fly but not being able to leap off. He kept up the delicious torment until she couldn't handle it any longer.

"Please. Oh, God, Caine. Please," she begged, not caring how desperate she sounded. "I need you inside me."

Digging his fingers into her hips, he lifted her pelvis up and in one swift thrust he filled her completely and ended her torment. Except as he stared hard at her, his lips parted, and she realized it was not the end but only the beginning of something she couldn't fully comprehend. She had the distinct sensation that Caine was about to take her someplace she had only dreamed in fervent and erotic dreams.

At first his pace was slow and measured. Drawing in and drawing out. Leisurely savoring each thrust. Her entire body felt like liquid heat. Melting inside out from Caine's passionate touch. Not before Caine had any man made her feel this fevered, this ravenous for sex.

And not just for sex, but for him. She'd never been this hungry for anyone before. It consumed her completely as he moved inside her, taking her, possessing her.

Sweat rolled down from his forehead and chest as he picked up his pace and drove into her again and again. The way her body was angled, she felt every single hard inch of him. Every nerve ending in her body flared, every part of her flesh burned.

But she didn't want to climax like this. She craved

his skin touching hers. She needed to hold him, kiss him and taste him when she came. Nothing would please her more than that.

Lifting her hands, she covered his on her hips, pulling at his fingers. "I need to touch you," she panted. "I want your body against mine."

Still sheathed deep inside, Caine entwined his fingers with hers and came down to the bed, covering her form with his. She wrapped her arms around him, welcoming him in, reveling in the warmth and security of his body. If she could die like this, she'd be no less satisfied.

Nuzzling into the side of her neck, Caine nipped at her chin as he buried his hands in her hair. Pulling her head back, he took her mouth feverishly. Tasting and sampling her. Nibbling at lips, darting his tongue in and out.

She felt the scrape of his teeth on her tongue and her lips. She wondered, not for the first time, what it would feel like if he bit her. She expected pain, but wondered if there was euphoric pleasure in it, too. How much rapture would he find in the act? A lot, she suspected.

"Bite me," she panted against his mouth.

His head came up, and he stared into her eyes. "What?"

She tore at the bandage on her neck, exposing the previous bite marks. "I want you to bite me. I want to feel your teeth on me. I want to know what it would feel like to be completely and utterly yours, if only for tonight."

He rested his forehead against hers. "I can't.

However much pleasure it would give me, it would bond us and turn you. That's something that can never be undone."

"I don't care," she murmured. "I want to be yours."

He pressed his lips to her forehead, then to her cheek, then down to her mouth. "You are mine, Eve. This, today, means everything. I will never forget it, or you." He took her mouth once more and drove into her again and again.

She raked her nails over his back, hanging on as he drove her up and up, continually. She felt like she was floating in a euphoric fog, unable to think, incapable of moving. She could only feel. Every nerve ending fired. Every muscle contracted.

And when he buried himself so deep she thought she would scream, she came in a fury of white blinding light and a symphony of sensory bombardment.

Biting down on her neck, but careful not to break her skin, Caine came only seconds after her.

She'd never experienced such a sensory overload before. It was as if she could feel everything Caine was feeling. She saw her own face in orgasmic delight as if looking down at herself. She could taste her skin, her sweat and lust on her tongue. And her smell, a mélange of spice, plums and vanilla permeated her nose. Flashes of blood and sex and flowers and food raced over and over in her head. And the feeling of love filled her heart to the brim. She'd never experienced so many emotions before, especially at once, in her life.

But she knew this was Caine's way of showing her

his true feelings for her. He didn't need to speak
those words for her to know that he loved her. It was
enough to her just to know it existed, and that it was
real. As real as his body was on top of hers.

Chapter 28

Caine kissed Eve on the back of her shoulder while he stroked his fingers up and down her arm. She was so damn beautiful, with the softest skin he'd ever felt. Her back was exquisite. Smooth and sleek. He'd come to realize that when he had flipped her over onto her stomach and made love to her again. And as he spooned her, nuzzling into her neck, just underneath the satin of her hair, he wanted to make love to her all over again. He hardened into steel just thinking about the delicious, naughty things he wanted to do.

His hand traveled lower down her hip and around to her belly, slipping lower to cup her liquid heat in his hand. A small moan escaped his lips when he felt how hot she was under his exploring fingers. He heard her sharp intake of air.

"Aren't you hungry?" she panted.

He nibbled on the back of her neck. "Only for you."

"You promised me food." She chuckled.

"I'll feed you, I promise," he vowed as he slipped one finger and then another into her. "Just give me, mmm, say ten minutes."

Laughing, she opened her legs and wrapped one over his, giving him complete access to her. Her other hand came up over her head and she buried her fingers in his hair pulling his face closer to hers. Turning, she found his mouth with hers. He could taste her surrender on his tongue. It was like ambrosia.

As promised, ten minutes later—more like twenty—Caine released his possessive hold on Eve and allowed her to roll out of his bed. She stood, then glanced over her shoulder at him. The look was sassy and sexy. A look, he knew, he would never forget.

"Do you have a robe I could wear? You seemed to have ripped my clothes in half."

He nodded toward the door. "There's one on the back of the door."

She padded across the room, took the black silk robe and slipped it on. As she tied the robe, she regarded him, her head slightly tilted. He knew that look. It was one that told him she was thinking too much.

She opened her mouth to speak, but Caine put his hand up to stop her. He wasn't ready to hear those words. Not yet. "Do you like spaghetti? I make an amazing tomato sauce."

She pursed her lips and nodded. "Sounds delicious."

Caine stood, walked to his dresser and grabbed a pair of boxer shorts. He slid them on, then padded over to where Eve watched and waited. Cupping her cheeks in his hands, he kissed her thoroughly. When he was done, he rested his head against hers.

"I'm not ready for you to go."

After a quick smile, she said, "I'm not ready *to* go."

"Good."

He released her and took her hand. They walked together down the hallway to the kitchen.

"Would you like some more wine?" he asked as he picked up the bottle of red. She nodded, and he filled her glass, handing it to her.

She took a sip and smiled, then slid on to the stool at the kitchen island. "Your kitchen is great. Do you cook often?"

He shook his head. "Not as often as I would like, and never for anyone. You are my first victim in a long while."

Her smile waned and she touched the side of her neck where he had clamped down on her flesh in the throes of passion. The skin was starting to turn red.

He reached for her hand and squeezed it. "Did I hurt you?"

"It's fine."

"You know why I couldn't bite you, right?"

She nodded, but he could see the embarrassment on her face. She was ashamed for asking him for such a thing, thinking it would have increased her pleasure and his. It would have, but the consequences were far too great.

"Turning someone is a huge deal, Eve. And not for—"

"A casual fling. I know."

He brought her hand to his mouth and pressed his lips there. "You are not a casual fling. Far from it."

"I understand. I never should have asked." She withdrew her hand and set it on the counter.

He hated seeing that look on her face. As though she had done something wrong, when it was, in fact, the exact opposite. She had done everything right.

"My wife died during the turn."

"Oh my God, Caine." She grasped his hand in hers. "I'm so sorry. I didn't mean—"

"It's all right." He gave her a small smile. "I've learned to accept it. But you have to know that is why I won't, and not because you are not important enough to me to warrant it." He met her gaze, trying to force her to see how he felt about her. How his heart ached just looking at her beauty. "Do you understand?"

She nodded. "Yes. I understand."

"Okay. Now, how about some food?" He slid his hand out from hers and walked toward the refrigerator.

"Sure. I'm starving." She turned toward the living room. "Is it okay if I sit out on your balcony? It looks like a gorgeous night."

"Sure. You get comfortable and I'll get the sauce cooking."

With a little smile, she went across the living room to the sliding glass door. She opened it and stepped out onto the deck, closing the door behind her. He watched her the whole time, enjoying the way she looked in his place, wearing his robe. He could get used to it.

He turned around and opened the refrigerator, grabbing some onions and tomatoes. Setting them on the chopping board, he slid out a knife and began to slice them up. The entire time he thought about Eve and the way she made him feel. His skin still tingled from their lovemaking. Despite not taking her blood, they had bonded and now it would be virtually impossible to forget her. Her scent, her taste, the look of her incredible body would forever be ingrained in his mind, on his soul.

On the eve of her return to San Antonio, he wasn't sure he could let her go.

Knife poised in the air, the shrill ring of the phone on the counter made him slip. The blade sliced across his finger. Sticking his bloodied finger into his mouth, Caine fumbled for the phone.

"Valorian."

It was Mahina. "Jesus Christ, Caine, I've been trying to get a hold of you for the past two hours."

"Monty's on call. I turned my cell phone and pager off."

"I guessed that."

"What's up?"

"Mel Howard escaped lockup."

A wave of ice surged up Caine's back. A sick sinking feeling made his stomach roil. He could hardly swallow the bile rising in his throat.

His eyes swung to the glass door of his balcony, a sense of dread washing over him. "How?"

"We don't know, but he's gone."

Before she could say anything else, Caine moved across the living room in a few long strides. Sliding open the door, he stepped out onto the deck.

The phone fell from his hand.

Eve was gone.

Wine dripped onto the stained wood deck from the overturned glass on a small metal table. A soft breeze blew across his face, bringing the smell of fear to his nose. Eve's fear. It was sharp and bitter. And fresh. She'd barely been gone five minutes.

He also detected another odor. Chloroform.

Panic overtook him. He jumped over the balcony railing and ran down to the street. He looked both ways for retreating vehicles. He saw the taillights of a car racing down his street and turning right. Possibly red. Possibly a sports car.

He ran back to the balcony, jumped the railing and picked up the phone. He could hear Mahina's impatient cries. "Caine? Caine! What the hell is going on?"

"Put out an APB on the suspect's car. I need the team over here immediately. Eve's gone. The bastard's taken her."

Chapter 29

Smacking her lips together, Eve tasted vile bitterness in her mouth. The hard, cold surface she had been laid on bit through the thin material of the robe she wore. She rolled over onto her back and slowly opened her eyes.

Nausea crested over her as she struggled to keep her eyes open. Everything was black. The tiny pinpoints of light she could determine swam in and out of focus, making her head swim and her stomach roil.

She rolled over onto her side again and clamped her eyes shut. Staying still, she took in slow, measured breaths, trying to will the nausea away. She had no luck.

Had she drunk too much wine? Is that why the

world was spinning like a top? Why she felt like her head was floating, detached from the rest of her body?

Confusion muddled her brain. She had no idea where she was. Hadn't she just been with Caine in his house? Wasn't he making her dinner?

Spaghetti. That was it.

Spaghetti and a delicious tomato sauce.

"Caine," she managed to croak. Her throat felt so dry and shriveled. Dehydrated. From the wine?

Her voice echoed back and a sense of dread surged over her, clenching her stomach even tighter.

She was definitely not in Caine's house.

Panic rushed through her and she tried to sit up. But she found her body wasn't obeying her. The best she could do was lift her head and peer around.

The dark still encompassed her, but she could make out a few details. The wall closest to her, made of cement or possibly stone, was gray with some darker patches scattered over it. Black paint, maybe? She could also see a thin layer of light glowing on the floor. Coming from under a door?

The smell of decay and mold wafted to her nostrils. It was an odor she'd experienced many times before. One of death and despair. The morgue. Was that where she was, in the morgue? Lying dead on a metal slab, and this was her transcended state of existence?

Shaking her head, she tried to sit up again. This time she managed to lift her arms before she collapsed back down. Moving her hands, she felt the surface beneath her. It was definitely cement and not steel. She couldn't be dead. She wouldn't be able to feel this much pain, would she?

"Caine," she called again, desperation cracking her voice.

A sharp creaking sound broke the dead silence around her. Shifting, she looked up and saw the light on the floor grow into a yellow rectangle. A shadowy outline filled the shape.

"He can't help you now, sweet thing."

She knew that voice. But from where? It tickled the back of her mind like a pinprick.

The shape floated closer to her along the floor like a black fog. Instinctively she shuffled backward in retreat, revulsion pooling in her mouth.

"It's just you and me for now, sugar."

A cold hand touched her forehead. She lifted her arms and tried to swat the contact away. It felt like Death himself had placed his hand upon her.

The familiar voice chuckled. "Hmm, so spirited. He's going to love that about you."

A finger traced her cheek, then down to her throat. She turned her head away, but his touch remained, eager and bitter. Then he circled her neck with his finger, pressing harder with each stroke.

"Maybe we can finish where we left off."

Blinking back tears, Eve struggled to keep from vomiting. She remembered now who the voice belonged to—Mel Howard. The murderous vampire who had attacked her outside his home.

"So pretty," he cooed as his hand wrapped around her throat. He squeezed tight cutting off her air.

Clawing at his hand, Eve tried to fend him off. But he was much too strong, and she realized now that she had been drugged with more than just chloroform. She could still feel the paralyzing effects of it wearing off. And judging by the horrid taste in her mouth, she had breathed in a lot of it.

She'd been kidnapped from Caine's deck. But how? Didn't she see Mel Howard in the police station in handcuffs? They had caught him. He was guilty of murdering that poor young girl and his accomplice in cold blood. Did they let him go?

Then she felt a sharp pinch just below her right ear. Within seconds, it felt like she was being sucked through a vacuum hose. He released his grip around her neck, but she still had trouble getting air.

She clawed at her throat, but soon her hands felt heavy, leaden and they fell away to the side of her head. Her arms stiffened like superglue drying. Instantly freezing in place. She tried to move her legs, but couldn't. The only thing she was capable of doing was shifting her eyes.

She was paralyzed.

Mel leaned down. She could feel his nose pressed against her cheek and his hot, rancid breath in her ear. "I'm so pleased that I get playtime with you, sweet thing." He rolled his tongue over her earlobe. "It's my reward for serving him so well."

Eve screamed. But nothing came out. She was incapable of opening her mouth. The sound just echoed around in her skull, bouncing around like a rubber ball, until she thought she'd go insane. Maybe she would. Then she could retreat into herself, away from what Mel was going to do to her.

She tried to clamp her teeth together when his hand trailed lower. But something else drew her attention. Shifting her eyes up, she swore she saw another shadow fill the yellow rectangle of light on the floor.

Chapter 30

"Where the hell is my trace evidence?" Caine paced the lab staff room, his hands clenched into tight fists. His team was watching him from various positions around the room. They had processed the scene, his home, quickly and respectfully, but now it was a matter of waiting for that evidence to be processed.

They had lifted Mel's prints from the deck railing, so they knew for sure he was the one who took Eve, and they discovered trace amounts of dirt on the deck. Other than that they had nothing to go on. So far, no reports had come back on the APB for his red sports car.

"It's coming, Chief. You know it takes time to do it right," Lyra said from her seat at the table.

"Why do you think he took her?" Mahina asked from her perch on the edge of the counter. "It would've been smarter for him to disappear. He could've crossed the city lines and gotten lost in San Antonio. We would've had a hard time tracking him there."

"Revenge maybe?" Jace offered. "To prove that he could."

"I'd like to know how the hell he got out," Caine growled, turning on Mahina.

"We don't know, Caine. It had to have been an inside job, though. Anyone in law enforcement would have access to the holding cells." She pushed away from the counter. "Including staff of this lab."

Caine stopped pacing and glared at her. "Are you accusing one of my team?"

"I'm not saying that."

"What are you saying?"

"That we have to look at every possibility."

Caine rubbed at his forehead where a massive migraine was pounding, making a valiant effort to break his skull in half. "Okay, what do you need?"

"Access to everyone on staff. I need to ask everyone where they were between five and eight last night."

"On a Sunday night most of the staff would've been at home."

"Then I'll need names and addresses."

Caine nodded. "I'll get the list. It's in my office."

Kellen slid off the counter where he'd been sitting silently, munching on day-old pizza. "Well, kids, I'm out of here. Looks like you have it all handled. Nothing I can do."

Caine glared at him. "No one's leaving until we find Eve."

Kellen put up his hand in defense. "Hey, I feel bad for the girl, it's a real shame, but it's not like I have a vested interest in her." He snorted. "I'm not the one nailing her."

Faster than anyone could blink, Caine gripped Kellen by the throat, heaved him up off the floor and slammed him onto his back on top of the table. The other vampire struggled, but it was pointless. Caine's strength was fueled by fury. There was no breaking his hold, however much the other vampire punched and scratched at Caine. He'd let go only if he wanted to.

Leaning down into Kellen's face, Caine sneered, "I could end you right now."

Mahina approached the table, her hands out in a calming gesture. "Caine, this isn't helping."

He ignored her. He wanted to hurt something, someone. Maybe then the pain of Eve's kidnapping would dissipate. Maybe it would somehow dampen the agony that tore through him since she'd been taken. Caine wasn't sure how much more he could stand before he completely lost his mind, and his soul. He felt fractured without her.

Kellen mumbled something, snapping Caine from his bloodlust rage. Releasing his grip a little, he leaned in closer to him.

"I'm sorry," Kellen rasped.

As Caine stared into the other vampire's eyes, he

saw a flash of regret. It was enough to snap him out of his fury and back to reality.

He released his hold and took a step away. His hands still shook with anger, but he reined it in. Not once had he ever physically harmed any member of his team. Until now.

Aided by Mahina and Jace, Kellen sat up and rubbed at his neck. He looked up and met Caine's gaze. "I'm sorry, Chief. I didn't realize."

Revulsion swirled in his stomach. Clenching his hands, Caine dropped his gaze and turned. He'd come so close to seriously hurting Kellen. Over fifty years ago, he had vowed not to use his power to harm another being. And he had snapped over something as harmless as a few careless words. Mean-spirited certainly, but words nonetheless.

What were his feelings for Eve doing to him?

Kellen slid off the table and approached Caine. He offered his hand to him. Sighing, Caine took it.

"I'm sorry for my stupid mouth. I didn't realize you had actually bonded with her. It won't happen again, Chief. I swear."

They shook hands.

"I apologize for nearly snapping your neck."

Kellen smiled and shrugged. "I'll live." Taking his hand back, Kellen shuffled out the door. "I'll go see if the trace lab is done."

When he was gone, Caine ran his hands over his face and through his hair. He couldn't believe what he'd almost done. His feelings for Eve would be the death of him—or the death of someone else.

Mahina placed her hand on his shoulder and leaned in. "Do you want me to see where Kellen was a few hours ago?"

Caine met her gaze. He could see the wheels turning inside her head. Unfortunately, the same wheels were spinning in his. Something had triggered Kellen's attitude toward Eve. He didn't want to consider it, but at this point he had to look into every possibility.

He nodded.

She squeezed his shoulder in understanding, then took a step back.

"I'll go get you that employee list, Mahina."

"Good idea."

Before Caine could leave, Lyra spoke. "Maybe he's trying to finish what he started." She peered around the room.

Caine knew that look. Her witchy senses were tingling. "You mean with this demon summoning?"

She nodded.

"He began the ceremony with Lillian, so now he wants to use Eve to finish it?"

She nodded again, her face growing pale.

Bile rose in his throat. He didn't want to consider it, but knew if he didn't he might miss something important in the evidence. That was all they had to go on.

"What would he need to do it properly?"

Chewing on her lip, Lyra said, "The second ceremony is a longer one. He'd need the blood from his first victim, another animal bone and time. A secluded place most likely and a stone dais. So, I'm thinking he must've had the place already picked out long ago."

Jace grunted. "I can't believe we're entertaining this notion. It's ridiculous. Demons don't exist."

"Whether they exist or not isn't the issue here, Jace," Lyra said. "The suspect believes in it."

"Lyra's right. We need to consider every possibility." Caine ran a hand through his hair and sighed. "Let's think of places where he could go. Secluded buildings or areas. And somewhere close. He'd want to do this quickly."

Looking around at the others, he knew what they were thinking. That it was already done. That Eve had already been sacrificed. But he knew it wasn't true. He would know if she was dead. Because of their bonding, he would feel if she was gone. A feeling of complete emptiness would invade his heart. So far, it hadn't. They still had time to find her. He *had* to find her.

Lyra stood. "I'll get a map of the downtown grid, from Twelfth Street to Digger and Moonglow Road to Fallen. There must be a few abandoned warehouses in the area."

Caine nodded.

Jace stood. "I'll help you, Lyra."

As they left the room to locate a map, Jace patted Caine on the shoulder. But before they got two steps out, Gwen came barreling into the room, paper rustling in her hands.

"Got the results, Chief," she panted, clearly out of breath.

Caine took the sheet and scanned the results. "Soil decomp and trace bits of grass."

"Decomp?" Jace questioned. "Where the hell would he have picked up that?"

"The dump?" Mahina offered.

Caine shook his head. "The landfill is pretty far out of the area. It's at least a forty-five-minute drive from here."

Rubbing his fingers at his temple, Caine pondered the evidence. The answer was there. It always was, if a person knew how to put it all together. So how did it go together? Decomp. Demons. Blood. Sacrifice.

Caine turned to Lyra. "What did you say he'd need for the ceremony?"

"Blood, an altar, someplace secluded and an animal bone to draw the symbols with."

"Animal bone. We found one at the last scene. Decomp. How about a slaughterhouse? Any near here?"

One by one they rushed into the analysis room. Caine sat at the computer and pulled up a map of Necropolis. In the search engine, he typed in *slaughterhouses*. Three possible results came up.

Excitedly, Lyra pointed to the screen. "Look. This one's on Nightspell and Digger."

"And it's been closed for years," Caine added.

Jace slapped Caine on the shoulder. "That's got to be it."

"Do you want me to send units to the other two locations?" Mahina asked.

Caine nodded. But now that they had a location, he

knew deep down inside it was the right place. He could sense it on several levels. When he closed his eyes and concentrated, he could feel Eve's pain and her fear. Thankfully, she was still alive. And waiting for him.

Hang on, Eve! I'm coming!

Chapter 31

Eve jerked awake. Something had jolted her out of her dreamless slumber. A sound. A thought. She wasn't sure. All she knew was that she was still on the hard cement floor struggling to stay alert and conscious. So far she wasn't doing very well with either.

Mel had injected her with something. Her neck still throbbed from the puncture wound. Vampatamine, she guessed, by the way her body moved like thick molasses, as if restrained by some unseen chains. And her mind was muddled and confused.

Time was irrelevant to her. She didn't know whether a minute had passed since last time she was awake, or a few hours. She knew that it couldn't have been any longer than six or seven hours as her stomach rumbled from hunger but didn't feel hollow.

Struggling to move, Eve jerked her shoulder and rolled onto her back. The motion made her nauseous, but she managed to keep the bile rising in her throat down. If she could just focus on something she'd be able to ride out the effects of the drug. As long as he didn't inject her again, she was sure it would wear off in a few more hours. Someone would find her before then, she hoped desperately.

Blinking her eyes repeatedly, she tried to take in more of the room. It was still dark, but she was starting to adjust to it. She was definitely in some sort of large empty room. A rancid odor was ingrained into the cement. She'd smelled something similar before, but couldn't place it.

Lifting her hands, she smoothed them over her form. She was still wearing the robe, and it was still done up, marginally, but it proved to her that Mel had not taken advantage of her. Not yet anyway. Gauging her body, she didn't feel anything wrong with it. No immediate pain radiated from having been violated. Maybe she'd be saved that agony.

She had a sense that he had been interrupted before he could do anything. As if someone else had entered the room. She'd seen another shadow on the floor, hadn't she? Shaking her head, she tried to remember.

But her memories were disjointed, fractured like glass shards scattered all over her mind's surface. When she tried to put everything back together, the

entire picture made no sense. It didn't fit. Either something was missing or there were too many pieces.

The sound of the door opening startled her. She
tried to see who had entered. It wasn't long before
she found out. Mel leered down at her. But there was
something wrong with his face. She couldn't exactly
say, but it seemed like his mouth had grown wider,
longer even. As if somehow his face had melted,
letting gravity do its work on his flesh. There were
also dark streaks over his chin, and across his cheeks.
Was it blood?

When he crouched down next to her, a distinct
metallic odor wafted over her and up her nose. It was
most definitely blood.

He licked his lips and snarled. "He told me to feed
before the ceremony. Said he didn't want me to inter-
rupt it with my voracious thirst for blood." Reaching
up, he gently touched her hair, rubbing the strands
between his fingers. The action reminded her of
Caine, and a sense of utter loss swept over her, tearing
at her heart. Tears filled her eyes. Oh God, she didn't
want to die. Not before having one more chance to tell
Caine. To tell him she was in love with him.

Mel trailed his fingers over her forehead, down
her nose and to her lips. "As if I would do that. The
summoning is more important than anything else."
He pushed his finger into her mouth. "Even a sweet
thing like you."

She wanted to bite down on his finger. To give him
one ounce of the pain that he had inflicted on his
victims. But she was too weak even to spit. Besides,

she had the foresight to consider what his blood might do to her. Could she turn? Hadn't she read that in one of the texts?

Sliding his finger out of her mouth, he brought it to his lips and rubbed her saliva over his flesh. Revulsion filled her, and she gagged. Turning her head, she spit up bile. There was nothing else in her stomach to bring up.

Shaking his head, Mel grinned. "Ah, what's the matter, bitch? Don't you feel well?" As he snickered, he put his hand on her breast, squeezing and pinching hard. "You feel good to me."

Clamping her eyes shut, Eve tried to pull away from his horrid touch. But she could do no more than arch her shoulder and slightly roll her hip. He laughed at her effort and continued to pinch and grab her flesh. Thankfully, the fabric of Caine's robe was a barrier between her skin and his, but she could still feel the iciness of his touch. It was as though someone had opened a window and a cold wind had blown through the room.

Flinching as if struck, Mel yanked his hand back from her body. He glanced over his shoulder nervously. "I'm doing it, Master. I was just playing a bit."

Eve rolled her head back and stared at Mel. Was he hearing voices? Or was that a whisper she had heard on the breeze that swept over her. Had someone spoken Mel's name?

Before she could consider it, Mel stood, walked around and stooped down by her head. He hooked his hands under her armpits and lifted her up. Her legs were like rubber and she couldn't support her own weight. She crumpled into his arms.

With a sigh that sounded like disgust, Mel grabbed her around the chest and began to drag her across the room. "I guess I gave you too much V."

A few feet more and they were at a doorway. Pale yellow light spilled through it. Not light from electricity, but a glow from several candles. He dragged her through the room.

"Won't matter, I guess. In an hour you're going to be dead and I'm going to be immortal."

While he dragged her across the cement, Eve could see her surroundings more clearly. They had entered a vast area, a warehouse-type structure. Some of the features she recognized as industrial. Long chains hung from the vaulted roof. On the end were hooks in varying sizes. They were in some sort of abandoned warehousing unit. She saw dirt, trash and what looked like hay on the floor as he pulled her along.

The rancid smell was stronger out here. But the air was also fresher. She could almost place it. Something from her childhood. A disturbing memory of when her father had taken her to a farm one summer. And she'd seen her first murder.

She was in a killing house, all right. The odor was one of animals, of blood and of death. She was in an old meat-processing plant, she now knew. And she was the animal on the chopping block.

Chapter 32

When Mahina pulled her cruiser into the barren stockyard of the old slaughterhouse, the first thing Caine noticed was Mel's red Pontiac sitting in front. He hadn't even made an effort to hide it. For some reason Caine found that vulgar. As if Mel was flaunting his crimes. Daring the authorities to arrest him.

Anger flared inside. Caine couldn't wait to get his hands on the murdering vampire. Mel had better pray that Eve was relatively unharmed; because if she wasn't, Caine knew he wouldn't be able to maintain his vow not to hurt another being.

After Mahina parked, she and Caine got out of her vehicle. The lab's SUV pulled up behind them. Jace and Lyra jumped out, both of them wearing flak jackets and carrying guns. As a rule, the OCU didn't possess weapons, but the baron had made an exception in this case, granting them all the power to carry while on duty.

Caine decided to forgo a gun, as he knew he'd be way too tempted to use it when he saw Mel Howard.

Mahina unholstered her weapon. "Okay, this is how it's going down. I go in first. Caine, you're behind me. Jace and Lyra come in when I give the go-ahead." She stared at Caine, her eyebrow raised. "Everyone clear on that?"

He nodded, but knew he couldn't promise her he wasn't going to rush in if he saw Eve. That was all he could think about—saving her.

Mahina moved forward. Caine followed close behind. Approaching the main service door, she stopped and checked the knob for a lock. There was none, so she slowly opened it. Entering gun first, Mahina stepped over the threshold. Once she was through, Caine moved into the dark abandoned structure. Neither one of them needed a flashlight to see.

The smell of new and old death hit him like a sledgehammer to the abdomen. He nearly doubled over from the intensity of the sensation. Closing his eyes, he tried to sense if the new death was Eve's.

He didn't think so, but he knew she was in trouble. He could sense her alarm and confusion swirling all around him. It was disjointed and incoherent. She must have been drugged. Vampatamine was his guess. He feared they didn't have much time.

After they passed the doorway, they entered what looked like a series of offices. The windows were broken, and the desks long gone. Just the dirt and trash of something long ago forgotten remained on the cement floors.

Once they passed the offices and ascertained there was no imminent danger, Mahina radioed to Jace and Lyra that it was safe to enter. Once done, she and Caine continued on into the open warehouse area.

Mahina stopped in her tracks, glanced over her shoulder at Caine and whispered, "I can smell the bastard."

"Me, too."

They continued walking side by side now. Caine had conveniently forgotten to stay behind. He couldn't now, even if he wanted to. His predatory instincts had kicked in. He had a vampire to hunt down.

As they moved farther into the warehouse, it became apparent quite quickly that there was no one else in the expansive room. There were no walls or structures to hide behind in the vast area. It was one large, open floor space. Probably when in use, it had been the shipping and receiving area of goods and merchandise.

The slaughterhouse was where they needed to go. That was where Mel would do his work. His summoning. Where the stink of death and decay already permeated the air like a cloying perfume.

Caine pointed to the far wall. Mahina nodded and picked up her pace. They were nearing a set of double doors. A faint yellow glow emanated from underneath the metal. Candlelight, most likely.

The odor of fear, Eve's fear, distinctive by the

licorice taste, intensified as they got closer. Caine pushed forward intent on crashing through the doors. Eve was calling to him. He was sure of it. She was waiting for him to come. He wouldn't fail her again.

Before he could, Mahina grabbed his arm, yanking him to a halt. "I can hear some chanting. Sounds like two voices."

"Are you sure?"

She screwed up her nose and tilted her head, then shook it. "No, but it's strange. I can hear him, but also this low-level hum just under his octave. Like a second voice, but not."

"I don't care if it's Balam himself having a sing-along with the bastard, I'm going in. Eve is still alive— I can feel it. But I'm not sure for how much longer."

Mahina let him go and nodded. "Okay, but stay behind me. We'll go in together—on three."

They both looked over their shoulders at Jace and Lyra as they crept along the side of the warehouse wall. Mahina put up her hand to tell them to stop where they were and to wait for them to move. They both nodded that they understood.

Resigned to being held back, Caine huddled up behind Mahina as she took a position in front of the double metal doors. Wrapping her hands around her gun, she counted, "One…two…three."

She kicked in the door and rushed through it. Caine was right behind her. If she had turned they would've been nose to nose, but she never got the chance to do that.

The sound of gunfire rang in Caine's ears even

before he knew what was happening. Mahina pushed him to the ground as she took two bullets. One in her right hand, and the other in her side.

Diving across the room, Caine watched as the detective fell to the floor, her weapon falling from her crimson-stained hand. Blood quickly drenched the side of her shirt. The side not protected by the Kevlar vest. It had been a lucky shot.

Finding refuge behind a turned-over metal filing cabinet, Caine surveyed the room and spied Mel standing by a makeshift stone altar, candles all around, with a gun in his hand. Behind him on the altar, blood stained the stone, dripping down the side. And Eve lay spread out on top, Caine's robe that she wore pulled open and her naked form glistening in the flickering light of the candles. Her arm hung lifelessly over the flat surface.

"You're too late, assholes! The deed is done." Mel laughed hysterically as he swung his weapon back and forth. Caine didn't think he was in control; the vampire was insane.

Clenching his teeth, Caine wanted to rush out and rip Mel's throat out with his bare hands. Tears sprang to his eyes. She couldn't be dead. She just couldn't. He would've felt it. He was sure he would've felt it deep inside his soul. He was too late. Again, too late to save the woman he loved. History had a nasty habit of repeating itself.

Glancing over the cabinet again, Caine caught sight of something that set his heart racing and his throat constricting with emotion. Movement from atop the altar.

He could clearly see the rise and fall of her chest. Eve's head turned to the side. Her eyes opened. They stared right at him, into his heart.

Ducking back down, Caine had to think and consider. If he rushed Mel, he could get shot and have no chance of saving Eve. But what other option did he have?

He glanced over at Mahina, as she still moved on the floor. She had managed to pull herself to the side behind a stack of wooden flatbeds. She was slumped over, but still alive. She looked up and met his gaze. She shook her head, letting him know she had no ideas.

Pressing his lips together, he tried to think of something else. Panic surged through him. If he wasn't quick enough, Eve would die.

The radio clipped to his collar crackled to life.

"Chief, I'm just outside the doors. I have a clear shot." It was Jace.

"Are you sure?" he whispered into the radio. "You might hit Eve." Glancing over his shoulder, Caine could see Jace's face in the crack between the double doors.

"I won't. Lyra has a smoke screen spell. It'll work, trust me."

Nodding, Caine gave him the thumbs-up.

On a count of three, Caine took a deep breath and watched as a thick layer of black smoke erupted from beneath the doors and moved across the room as if alive. Caine popped up from behind his metal shield and charged. At the same time, Jace burst through the doors and fired two shots at Mel. Both low and aimed at his legs.

Taken by surprise, Mel stumbled to the right and fired off a shot. But it was enough to afford Caine time to reach him and kick the gun from his hand. But that didn't put Mel down.

Growling like a wild animal, he launched himself at Caine, his hands out like claws, making a grab for Caine's throat. As he jumped, his boots knocked over a couple of candles around the altar. They fell over and rolled across the floor into a corner.

Sidestepping, Caine landed a punch to the side of Mel's head, right to the temple. This time he was stunned and fell to one knee. Taking advantage, Caine grabbed him by the hair and kneed him in the face. Not giving him any time to react, Caine dragged Mel across the floor and put him on the ground. Caine kneeled over him and punched him two more times in the face.

"We got you, Mel. You're going to jail for the rest of your unnatural life."

That was when he started laughing.

Caine stared down at him incredulously.

"You'll never take me. My soul is reserved for *him*."

Caine watched in horror as blood erupted from Mel's mouth like a geyser. He bent down and tried to pry Mel's lips apart. The vampire convulsed on the floor, clawing at Caine's hands. Finally, Caine got his mouth open but it was too late.

Mel had bitten off his tongue and was choking on the blood.

In a matter of seconds, Mel's eyes rolled back in his head and he sagged onto the cement floor, dead.

With no further thoughts for Mel, Caine pushed to his feet and rushed over to the stone dais. Eve blinked up at him, her eyes glassy with tears. He stroked her hair and murmured to her. "I'm here, Eve. You're safe now." Leaning over, he pressed his lips to her forehead. Her skin was cold and clammy. He ran a hand over her neck and found her pulse. It was there, but weak. Had the bastard given her too much V?

After wrapping her back up in his robe, he slid an arm under her legs and around her waist just as fire erupted in the corner of the room. A few lit candles had found their way over to two jerry cans of gasoline. Suddenly Caine became aware of the smell of fuel all around them. He glanced down at the cement floor around the stone altar. It was slick with gasoline. The place was going to go up into flames any minute. With his senses so focused on Eve, he had missed the obvious odor. A stupid error on his part.

Standing up, he cradled Eve in his arms, pressing her close to his chest. When he turned, he saw Jace and Lyra tending to Mahina on the ground. Blood stained the cuff of Jace's jeans. He'd obviously been shot.

They both glanced up at him as he ran past, Eve safe in his arms.

"Time to go," he grunted. "The place is going to blow."

One on either side of Mahina, Jace and Lyra lifted her up and followed Caine out of the slaughter room.

As he rushed out of the building, Caine kept

looking down at Eve, making sure she was still there, still real. Her breathing was shallow and he worried that she wouldn't make it.

By the time he walked out of the warehouse, a few other police cruisers had surrounded the building, their red and blue lights flashing like beacons. A fire truck was wailing in the distance.

Eve moved in his arms and he looked down at her. She smiled up at him and opened her mouth to speak. She mumbled something that he couldn't quite hear.

He leaned his head down closer to her mouth. "What was that, honey?"

"Did you get him?"

He nodded. "Yeah, baby. Mel's dead. He can't ever hurt you again."

"The other one, too?"

"There was no one else there."

Her brow wrinkled in thought. He'd seen that look of concentration so many times before. She was thinking hard about something.

"Are you sure?" she rasped.

He nodded. "You're safe, baby."

Nodding, she snuggled into his chest and smiled. "You came for me. Just as I dreamed."

Tears filled his eyes. "I'll always come for you, Eve. No matter what."

"I love you," she rasped, and her eyelids fluttered closed.

His heart convulsed with emotion. An emotion he hadn't felt in a long time. One he thought he'd never feel again. Smiling, he pressed his lips to her forehead and whispered, "I love you, too."

But she was already unconscious and didn't hear a thing.

Chapter 33

"*He's coming for you, sweet thing.*"

Eve bolted straight up from where she lay. Panic gripped her tight as she surveyed her surroundings. Swiveling her head back and forth, she tried to figure out where she was.

The room was white-walled and she was in a bed with metal railings. A machine beeped beside her, and a tube ran out of her arm. *Hospital.* She was safe and sound in a hospital.

Caine slept in a chair next to her bed. Slumped over to one side, his face was slack. His blue shirt was streaked with blood. She remembered everything. Caine had come for her. He had rescued her just as she knew he would.

Leaning back into her pillows, she let out a deep breath and cried.

Her entire body convulsed with emotion as she let it all out. All her trepidation, her despair and longing seeped out in long wailing sobs.

Caine jerked awake and shot forward in his chair. He reached for her hand. "What's the matter? Are you in pain? I'll call the nurse."

She shook her head, unable to form any coherent words.

Reaching up, he stroked his hand over her forehead and hair. "You're all right, baby. You're safe."

She couldn't respond. When she opened her mouth, more sorrowful moans escaped. She could hardly breathe from the pressure on her lungs. Her head throbbed with the intensity of her distress. Instead of fighting it, she succumbed to it. Allowed it to pull her under like a wave rolling across sand.

Caine held her through it, softly murmuring to her, gently stroking her hair and her cheeks.

She had survived death. That's all she could think of. That's all that raced through her mind. She knew she had been so close to her end that she could still feel the icy press of the blade on her chest, on her neck, like a premonition of how it would feel in the afterlife. Caine had arrived just in time. A few more moments and she would've been dead.

Reaching up, she buried her hand in his hair and pulled him close. She needed to feel his warmth, the heat of his body against hers. Maybe then she'd stop shaking.

He must have discerned her desperate need for him. He stood, and slid in next to her on the bed. He wrapped an arm under her neck, one around her waist and pulled her tight to him, nestling his head on top of hers.

He held her like that, close, firm and warm until the last of her sobs trembled past her lips, until the last quiver of fear passed over her skin.

Nuzzling into his chest, just under his chin, Eve sighed. It felt so right being with him like this. She never wanted to move, but knew that soon she'd have to do just that. Nothing lasted forever. Especially not something that felt so damn good, and so perfect. Something that their different societies would never let them have.

"Am I crushing you?" His voice was so quiet and low, she barely heard him.

She shook her head, and wrapped her arm around his waist, pulling him even closer.

Chuckling, he ran a hand up and down her back. "I'll take that as a no."

"I don't want to move. It's perfect right here."

He hugged her tight, and pressed his lips to her head. She could hear him take a ragged breath, and then let it out. He was about to say something. And she was sure it was something she didn't want to hear. Not now. Maybe not ever.

She clenched her hands into his back. "Please don't speak. I…I couldn't handle hearing those words now."

"Eve…"

She shook her head, and then looked up into his face. "Just kiss me. For now. Just kiss me."

And he did.

Leaning down, he covered her mouth with his. At first, it was gentle, soft, testing. Then it turned feverish, like a raging inferno of emotion.

He took her, sampling her lips with his teeth and tongue. She could feel the sharp point of his fangs as they scraped over her bottom lip. But she didn't care. All she wanted right now was Caine. And everything that went with him.

Streaking her hands over his back, she hungered for the feel of his warm flesh. The IV tube in her hand pulled as she moved her left arm, but she didn't care. That pain was insignificant compared to what she felt right now with Caine next to her, his heart racing, his breath shallow with desire.

Darting her palms under the hem of his shirt, she found the hard muscles of his chest and the soft stripe of hair that lined his sternum down to his trousers. The memory of tracing that line with her tongue flooded her mind and her senses. She wanted to feel that passion again.

She trailed her fingers down and clasped the button on his pants. With a skilled flick of thumb and forefinger, Eve popped it open.

Caine groaned as she touched him. The heavy weight of his erection felt so damn good in her palm. Life affirming.

"Eve," he moaned. "We shouldn't…"

"Yes, we should."

She rolled him over onto his back. His eyes were wide as she tore at the buttons on his shirt. But he must have sensed her need to control the situation, because he offered no help.

In seconds, she parted the cotton of his shirt, and ran her hands over his chest. She circled his nipples with her thumbs. And matched him moan for moan when she pinched and pulled at his taut flesh.

Another time she might've prolonged his pleasure, drawn it out, torturing him with each stroke. But right now she needed the affirmation of life and passion. She needed to fill herself up with everything that was good in the world to forget the evil she had faced.

Kneeling beside him, she made short work of his pants and boxer shorts, having them down to his ankles in seconds. His erection was hard like steel. She loved the feel of him in her hand. As she stroked him, she watched his face. Every flinch, every grimace sent shivers down her body. She loved that she could make him hunger for her so intensely.

Hiking up her gown, she straddled him, hovering above his erection. With one fluid move she sunk down on him, filling her slick channel with his hot flesh.

"Oh God, Eve," he moaned as she started to rock up and down.

Bracing her hands on his chest, Eve moved, sliding up and down on Caine. With every stroke, she clenched her jaw, already feeling the orgasm building inside. Heat flooded her body. Flutters of pure ecstasy radiated over the entire length of her form. From her head to her toes, she could feel…everything: the soft breeze floating in the room, the way Caine bunched and flexed his muscles inside her, the sound of his labored breathing and the smell of his skin.

She would remember it. Nothing could take that from her.

Moving faster with more deliberate actions, Eve fell forward, covering Caine's chest. She wrapped her hands around his head and buried her fingers into the silk of his hair.

His fingers dug into her hips, and she knew he was close to coming. As was she.

She nuzzled his chin with her lips, moving up to find his mouth. She kissed him with everything she had, everything she was.

He moved his hands up to her hair. Entwining his fingers, he pulled her head back to stare into her eyes just as he thrust into her so deep, as deep as her soul, and found release.

She found it at the exact same time.

Chapter 34

As Caine walked down the sanitized white hallway of the South Shadowwood Hospital, his shoes squeaking with each step, he glanced down at the white lilies in his hand and thought they were a pathetic gesture of his true feelings.

Wishing he'd thought of it sooner, Caine had snuck from her room when she finally fell back asleep. He hoped the flowers would make her smile again.

Eve lay in a bed a few feet away, recovering from her ordeal. Thankfully, once Caine had got her into an ambulance, they were able to stabilize her. When they got to the hospital, the doctor had been able to flush her system of the Vampatamine. The doctor told him a half hour more and she would not have made it.

He had stayed at her bedside for six hours, holding her hand, and eyeing the machine hooked up to her chest that monitored her vitals. Every blip and beep made him flinch with alarm. He'd seen countless people, even close friends, in hospitals fighting one thing or another. But nothing had affected him like this. No one had gotten into his mind and soul like Eve had.

When she had woken and reached for him, frantic for his touch, his heart had nearly shattered by the impact of her passion, by the impact of her. Their union had been powerful. Something he would never forget.

She had possessed him utterly.

As he approached the door to her room, he paused. He could hear someone speaking to her. Not a voice he recognized at first.

He peered around the corner and spied a tall, older Hispanic man standing at the foot of Eve's bed, his hands clasped firmly in front of him.

Captain Morales.

Now that he'd seen the man, Caine recognized the voice. He had phoned Eve's boss the moment she was out of danger at the hospital. He didn't realize that the man would come all this way to see her. Caine's respect for the man increased tenfold.

"I'll see that you get that pay raise when you come back to work," Caine heard Captain Morales say. "But make sure you take your time, Eve. You take all the time you need to get better and…put all this behind you." He paused, and then continued. "We have a good psychologist on staff if you need to talk to someone."

Caine heard her sigh. "I'm okay. I just need a few days."

"Well, once we get you into a real hospital with a real doctor, you can make that decision."

"This is a real hospital, Hector. Dr. Woodward is a real doctor. He even went to Harvard Medical School."

The captain huffed. "I'm just saying."

"I know what you're saying. And you're wrong."

Caine could hear some rustling, and he imagined Eve was trying to sit up and assert herself, even from the confines of a hospital bed. He had to smile at that. She had a lot of spunk.

"The people here are just people, Hector. People with strange and wonderful gifts. Gifts we may not understand, but that doesn't make them any less human. I figured that out big-time."

"If you had been with our crime scene team, none of this would've happened. I would never have let you get hurt. That vampire, Caine Valorian, has a lot to answer for."

Leaning against the wall, Caine tried not to react. But the captain was right, he did have a lot to answer for. There wasn't a minute that went by that he didn't blame himself for what had happened to Eve. If only he had sent her home when he should have, instead of selfishly holding on to her. It was his desire for her that nearly cost her her life.

He was a fool to believe that they could work past their differences. There were too many.

"This was not Caine's fault, Hector. That man is

one of the best crime scene investigators I have ever met. So please don't speak about him like that. He may be a vampire, but he is more human than most men I've known."

His heart swelled. If only she knew how much it truly meant to him to hear those words from her lips. To know that she would defend him. Oh, how wonderful they could've been together. If only…

"Well, Mr. Bask has already informed me that Valorian will be on a tight leash from now on. I think his investigation days are numbered."

Caine's pager took that moment to vibrate in his pocket. He didn't have to hazard a guess to know whose number would be on display. He guessed he now knew why the baron had been paging him all day. To ream him a new one.

Well, Caine figured, the baron could wait a little while longer for that pleasure.

Clearing his throat, he stepped into the room. Eve's smile blossomed the moment she saw him. And his heart skipped a few beats. Even in a green hospital gown, her hair everywhere, she took his breath away. She was a radiant beacon to the darkness of his soul.

"Caine," she breathed.

He gave her a little smile and bowed his head. "I see you are feeling better."

"Yes, thank you."

He neared the bed and handed her the flowers. She brought them to her nose. "Lilies. How did you know they were my favorite?"

He tapped his head. "My psychic abilities."

She hid her smile behind the blossoms of the white flowers. "Caine, this is Captain Hector Morales." She nodded toward the captain standing stiffly at the end of the bed.

Caine turned to the man and offered his hand. The captain took it and shook it briefly. "Yes, we've spoken on the phone." Releasing his hand, Caine swiveled back toward Eve. "I just came to see how you were doing before they…shipped you home. The team sends their regards. Even Jace seemed a little misty at your leaving."

She smiled, but he could see it did not reach her eyes. Motioning to Captain Morales, she said, "Could you give us a few moments please, Hector?"

The captain hesitated as he glanced at Caine. Then nodded and left the room.

He felt like his legs were leaden. He so much wanted to go to her, soothe her, take all her pain and suffering away with the stroke of his hands but he couldn't. Last night had been special. But it would never be the same between them again. They had their time together. And now it was the end.

She set the flowers on the side table. Shuffling a little, she tried to sit up more. Caine moved to her side, and helped her, placing another pillow up behind her back.

"Thank you."

"You're welcome," he responded as he took a step away.

Sighing, she brought her hands up and rubbed

them over her face. "Oh God, I don't want to do the polite thing, Caine. I really don't."

"Let's not then."

She glanced at him sideways and smiled in her little way. It nearly brought tears to his eyes. His heart clenched as if it was in a metal vise.

"You mean a lot to me." Tears started to brim in the corners of her gorgeous eyes.

He took a step closer and grabbed her hand in his, clenching it tight, afraid to let go, but knowing he must. "I feel the same, Eve. You are an amazing woman."

"But…" she breathed, as a teardrop rolled down her cheek.

Caine nodded. "But…"

She squeezed his hand tight, then let go, pulling it away and setting it alongside her leg. "Don't forget me."

"I won't." He paused then surveyed her face. She was so damn beautiful inside and out. A woman with guts and determination. A woman he could never forget in ten lifetimes. A woman he loved as the moon loved the night. Connected eternally. "I can't."

Wiping at her tears, she nodded and leaned back into her pillows. "Take care of yourself. I'd say don't work too hard, but I know it would be wasted on you."

He chuckled. "You, too."

Chewing her lip, she nodded at him again. He could see her struggle to maintain her emotions. Not wanting to break down in tears in front of him. If only she knew that that would be all it took for him to change his mind and not let her go. But he was too stubborn to tell her so.

With a final tip of his head, he turned and started toward the door. Knowing he did more than just leave the room. He was leaving a big part of himself behind. A part he hadn't realized he was missing to begin with.

He couldn't do it. He had to try.

He paused in the doorway, then swiveled around. "Do you want to go back to San Antonio?"

"What?"

He coughed into his hand, nerves making his throat constrict. "We work fairly well together, don't we?"

A small smile curved her lips. "Yes, I suppose. What are you suggesting?"

He moved toward her bed, his confidence building with each step. "A joint project of sorts."

"Uh-huh, I'm listening."

"Well, we both know that human and Otherworlder relations are strained. Working together as a team on this case, I believe, helped smooth those relations a bit." When he neared her side, he took her hand. "Just think what we could continue to do together."

She lifed her brow, her lips curling up. "Together. As in, a team?"

He nodded.

"Here in Necropolis?"

He nodded again.

"For how long?"

He lifted her hand to his moth, and pressed his lips to the back, nibbling on her smooth skin. "How about forever?"

Tears welled in the corners of her eyes. "Are you sure?"

"I love you, Eve. And I don't want to go another minute without you at my side." Leaning forward, he kissed her lips. "How is that for being sure?" he whispered against them.

She wrapped her arms around him and pulled him close. "I love you, too. You mean more to me than any man before."

Weaving his hands through her hair, Caine brought her mouth to his. He kissed her with everything he had, everything he was. He needed her to know that she had become the most important thing to him. More important than the lab, more important than any case.

With one last nibble on her bottom lip, he rested his head against hers and sighed.

"What do you think Hector and Baron Bask will say about this?" Eve asked, a playful grin on her face.

"They're both political animals, they know a good move when it's presented to them. I won't give either of them a chance to say no." He smiled. "I can be very persuasive." He kissed her again.

"Am I interrupting?" A voice sounded from the door.

Groaning, Caine glanced over his shoulder at Mahina as she leaned casually against the door frame. "Yes, in fact, you are."

"Good. My work here is done." She grinned.

"Shouldn't you be in a hospital bed, too?"

She chuckled. "Damn, Valorian, they were just lead. I've had cat scratches worse than that. What about you? Are you up for another case?"

"What's up?"

"We have another DB. Washington and Twenty-third Street."

Eve sat back and sighed. Keeping her gaze, Caine raised his hand and set it on her cheek. He ran his thumb over her lips. They were too soft to leave, too inviting to resist. He could imagine a lifetime of tasting them, and he didn't want to waste one single moment for that chance.

"Call Monty. I'm taking the day off."

"That's a first," Mahina remarked.

"Yup." Caine smiled. "But it won't be the last." Leaning over, he captured Eve's mouth and swallowed down her sigh of relief.

He knew Mahina said something before she left, but he didn't hear it. All that he could discern, all that mattered, was the sound of Eve's heart as it thumped in perfect rhythm with his own.

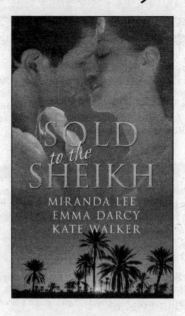

FREE!

2 Books
and a surprise gift!

We would like to take this opportunity to thank you for reading this Mills & Boon® book by offering you the chance to take TWO more specially selected titles from the Intrigue series absolutely FREE! We're also making this offer to introduce you to the benefits of the Mills & Boon® Book Club™—

- ★ FREE home delivery
- ★ FREE gifts and competitions
- ★ FREE monthly Newsletter
- ★ Exclusive Mills & Boon Book Club offers
- ★ Books available before they're in the shops

Accepting these FREE books and gift places you under no obligation to buy, you may cancel at any time, even after receiving your free shipment. Simply complete your details below and return the entire page to the address below. You don't even need a stamp!

YES! Please send me 2 free Intrigue books and a surprise gift. I understand that unless you hear from me, I will receive 4 superb new titles every month for just £3.19 each, postage and packing free. I am under no obligation to purchase any books and may cancel my subscription at any time. The free books and gift will be mine to keep in any case.

19ZEF

Ms/Mrs/Miss/Mr ....Initials ....

Surname .... **BLOCK CAPITALS PLEASE**

Address ....

....

....Postcode ....

Send this whole page to:
UK: FREEPOST CN81, Croydon, CR9 3WZ

Offer valid in UK only and is not available to current Mills & Boon Book Club subscribers to this series. Overseas and Eire please write for details. We reserve the right to refuse an application and applicants must be aged 18 years or over. Only one application per household. Terms and prices subject to change without notice. Offer expires 31st August 2009. As a result of this application, you may receive offers from Harlequin Mills & Boon and other carefully selected companies. If you would prefer not to share in this opportunity please write to The Data Manager, PO Box 676, Richmond, TW9 1WU.

Mills & Boon® is a registered trademark owned by Harlequin Mills & Boon Limited.
The Mills & Boon® Book Club™ is being used as a trademark.